PARANORMAL

ROMANCE#1

Compiled & Edited by

D. Kershaw | Maggie Pawsey | S.N. Graves

Also available and coming soon from Black Hare Press

DARK DRABBLES ANTHOLOGIES

WORLDS

ANGELS

MONSTERS

BEYOND

UNRAVEL

APOCALYPSE

LOVE

HATE

OCEANS

ANCIENTS

BHP WRITERS' GROUP SPECIAL EDITIONS

STORMING AREA 51

EERIE CHRISTMAS

BAD ROMANCE

TWENTY TWENTY

OTHER VOLUMES

DEEP SPACE

WHAT IF?

KEY TO THE KINGDOM

DEEP SEA

BEYOND THE REALM

Twitter: @BlackHarePress

Facebook: BlackHarePress

Website: www.BlackHarePress.com

Cover design	Dawn Burdett	www.dmburdett.com
Formatting	Ben Thomas	www.blackharepress.com
Editing	D. Kershaw	www.blackharepress.com
	Maggie Pawsey	
	S.N. Graves	www.sngraves.com
Read Team	David Green	davidgreenwritercom.wordpress.com
	Jennifer Hatfield	jhatfieldauthor.wixsite.com/website
	Jodi Jensen	jodijensenwrites.wordpress.com
	Lyndsay Ellis-Holloway	authorlyndseyellisholloway.webador.co.uk
	Stacey Jaine McIntosh	www.staceyjainemcintosh.com

TABLE OF CONTENTS

MIDNIGHT ALLURE
By Zoey Xolton

Ellia closed her eyes and took three deep, steadying breaths as her heart thundered in her chest. *He was still there.* Dark and brooding, almost at one with the shadows. Torn between the instinct to flee and her inexplicable desire to stay. On the knife-edge of fear and curiosity, she made her decision.

"Who are you?" she whispered.

A flash of brilliance in the night as he smiled, stalking towards her like a cat.

She clenched her fists by her sides, willing herself to stop trembling. Everything about him screamed *predatory*, but as he stepped into the moonlight, something within urged her to take an involuntary step forward.

"Vexen," he said in a voice that dripped with seduction and promise. The sort of tantalising promise that came with a price. "And what is your name, Kitten?"

Ellia swallowed hard, willing herself to be bold.

"My name—" she faltered. "My name

is Ellia."

His lithe form was terrifyingly close; his crimson eyes glittered, drinking her in from head to toe. He circled her, smelling her hair, trailing his smooth, cold fingers over the sensitive skin of her warm throat. "You're trembling," he said too softly into her ear. "Why do you fear me, little cat?"

Ellia bit the inside of her lip and drew in a sharp breath. "You're too beautiful to be *real*."

His sanguine gaze seemed to bore through her flesh and straight into her soul. He took another step closer. She could feel him, ice and fire, all at once. "Touch me; see that I am real," he coaxed.

Ellia raised an uncertain hand and laid it upon his chest. Solid and cold…but *real!*

His chest rose and fell beneath her shivering fingers. Her eyes darted up to meet his, but he wasn't looking at her. His gaze was fixed firmly past her, scrutinising the house on the hill, beyond.

"Someone's coming," he said.

"It's my Nan. She doesn't like me being out after dark."

"And for good reason," Vexen replied.

Ellia's brow furrowed as she searched his face for an answer. "What reason?"

"Isn't it obvious? She's afraid of losing you."

"Losing me?"

Vexen tucked her hair behind her ear, his hand lingering at her neck.

"I have a fascination with the women of your line, Ellia. Something in your blood calls to me, has done for centuries. Every Williams woman has seen me, known me...loved me."

Ellia took a step back towards the lake, shaking her head slowly. "I don't understand."

"She knows you're drawn to my allure. She's afraid you will succumb to me, thus ending the Williams line."

Ellia opened and closed her mouth, words and questions half forming. Her Nan's shadow stretched across the green hillside, the yellow porch light illuminating her from behind. She turned her attention back to Vexen, only to find him gone.

She spun around in a slow circle, crestfallen. "Vexen?" she whispered, already knowing there would be no reply...but that he'd return for her the following night, as sure as the sun would rise in the morning.

First published Darkly Ever After, Blood Song Books,2020

BLACK BEAR
By Vonnie Winslow Crist

When she rounded the bend in the trail, Dani spotted a bear digging at the roots of a tree stump. She stopped walking so suddenly, the bear-bells attached to her backpack jangled and her hiking boots kicked a handful of pebbles off the path and down a rocky embankment to her left. The creature responded to the noise by lifting his head, grunting, then twitching his ears.

Surprised by the enormous size and close proximity of the animal, Dani inhaled quick, shallow breaths. She'd always prided herself on being prepared for anything, but all the wildlife fact sheets she'd read hadn't accurately described the long curving claws on each of the bear's paws. Those claws were designed for ripping open logs to expose insects, tearing into earth to find tasty roots, overturning rocks to uncover reptiles and amphibians, shredding carrion, and scratching bear-sign on the trunks of trees. She hoped they wouldn't be used on her.

Stay calm and don't run, she reminded

herself. Running would excite the bear's natural chase instinct, so she needed to back away slowly.

As Dani took a couple of steps back, the bear stood upright on his hind legs.

He's just trying to get a better look, she thought. Though, to be entirely factual about the situation, bears rely on their sense of smell more than eyesight, so he was probably trying to figure out where this new smell was coming from.

Don't look him directly in the eyes, she reminded herself. *He'll think it's a threat.* And since she'd already invaded the animal's personal space, any additional threatening behaviour was likely to result in a charge.

Forgetting the steep drop-off to her

left, Dani took another step backwards and found herself teetering on the edge of the embankment.

The bear huffed a cloud of white smoke—water vapor, really, caused by the meeting of warm breath and cold air. Next, it woofed, dropped to all fours, and ran towards her.

Just then, Dani's feet slipped out from under her and she fell to her stomach. Fighting the weight of her backpack plus the gravelly, icy hillside, she grabbed at rocks and small bushes in an effort to avoid tumbling twenty or thirty meters down to the next level spot in the trail. The bear was only about two meters away when Dani realised her vulnerable predicament and surrendered to gravity.

LOCKDOWN PNR #1

The last things she remembered before blackness enveloped her were crashing through the brush and early snow, bouncing over fallen logs, slamming into the base of an oak tree, and seeing the face of the bear looming over her.

***

As Dani regained consciousness, she heard was greeted by the squeak of a faucet turning on, the whoosh of water, and the clank of a kettle being placed on a gas stove burner. She tried to speak, but her mouth felt like it was filled with cotton.

"Give yourself a minute," said a deep voice. "You've had quite a tumble. You're lucky to be in one piece."

She opened her eyes, squinting at the winter sunlight streaming through the window over the sink. A large man with black hair, beard, and moustache stood by the stove watching her.

"Water," she managed to squawk.

"Here you go," said the man as he helped her sit upright.

Even through the dark flannel shirt he wore, Dani noticed how muscular his arms were. And there was a pleasant woodsy smell to him, like he'd just come in from chopping firewood.

He held a mug to her lips. She swallowed several mouthfuls of water, then opened her eyes wide. What if it contained poison or drugs?

As if he read her thoughts, the man

smiled and took a drink from the mug Dani had just sipped from.

"Best well water in these parts."

He stood and extended his hand. "Garth Underwood, researcher, photographer, nature writer, and your neighbour."

"Neighbour?"

"Yes, indeed. You live up near the main road, but if you drive to the end of Turkey Run Lane and take the driveway to the right, you'll end up here." Garth spread his arms wide.

"How do you know where I live?" asked Dani uneasily. Maybe this Garth character wasn't the gentle giant he seemed to be. Maybe he was a stalker. And how had he found her? Against safety protocol, she'd been hiking alone. The only other creature on that hillside besides Dani had been the bear.

"I've seen you picking up your mail." He paused, studied the back of his hands.

Dani followed his gaze. She couldn't help but notice how hairy the backs of his hands were.

"And you've waited on me down at the Lakeside Restaurant," he added looking at her with kind, brown eyes.

"Oh!" Dani glanced away and tried to remember seeing Garth before today. She vaguely recalled him sitting alone near a window.

"Don't worry if you can't remember me." He shrugged. "Not many people do. I kind of blend into the woodwork."

Before she could think of a reply, Garth strode to the stove, removed the now whistling tea kettle, dropped teabags into two mugs, and poured boiling water into the pottery containers. After setting the kettle back on a burner, he turned towards Dani and asked, "Sugar? Honey? Milk?"

"A little honey. No milk or sugar."

"That's the way I like it." He grinned at her as he scooped a spoonful of the golden liquid into each mug. "I'm a great fan of honey. I think I could eat it every day—honeycomb and all!"

Dani returned his grin. Garth Underwood was quite likable. She wondered why she had never noticed him before. She took the tea from his hand.

"Delicious!" she said after tasting the

honey-sweetened brew.

"I agree." Garth took a gulp of the steaming liquid and watched her.

There was something familiar about his eyes. Maybe she did remember him from the Lakeside Restaurant.

"I think I'm remembering you."

"Really?" He leaned closer.

The smell of woods, berries, and earth was almost overwhelming. Her thoughts returned to today's hike. What had he been doing in the woods? Walking alone, perhaps taking photographs of this year's first snowfall? Had Garth heard her tumbling down the hillside, or had he seen it? And what of the bear? She was certain the creature had been staring down at her when she passed out.

"Did you actually see me fall?"

He nodded. "And I tried to get to you in time to catch you."

She shook her head. "No one could have reached me before I fell but the bear."

"I know."

"I don't understand." But even as she uttered the words, Dani recognised the kind, brown eyes as the eyes of the black bear.

"I didn't mean to scare you then, or now," said Garth as he took her hand in his.

She gasped as the scent of forest filled her nostrils and the warmth of Garth's hand made her want to lean closer. Dani thought of the day moon faintly shining in this morning's sky. It had been full.

"And the best part," whispered Garth

as gently, ever so gently, he bit her. "We both love honey."

First published Morpheus Tales: Ethereal Tales Issue, 2014

DOLL PARTS
By Ximena Escobar

"I won't talk about the past anymore," she said. "I'm only talking about what will happen from now on."

Bryan watched her lips move as she talked, her thumb caressing the edge of the seat in front. The flakes of her skin from biting it so much. The little white mark on her nail. He listened but drifted away in fond memories of her—he knew what she was going to say, anyway. He always loved that about her. Her drive to make the best out of every situation.

"I'm using this pain to make something wonderful."

LOCKDOWN PNR #1

He placed his hand on her hand, like he had so many times before. Her masculine hands. Creative hands for making wonderful things. Like her saddest smile.

She looked out the bus window. She looked at the foam peeping through the torn seat cover. She looked up at the dangling handles, defying her tears. It helped her to imagine bus-leather and yellow foam dress. The handles swayed with the bus stopping. She clasped the seat in front—composed, just then, by the physicality of inertia. By the loud door opening. By the loud woman who obviously knew the driver and wanted everybody to know it, laughing her way off.

"He doesn't see me… It's bad enough that he won't look at me, but he doesn't even *perceive* me in the periphery. It's sad, because I can still love that about him, you know? That he's decided. I always admired how he can decide so bluntly, separate the wheat from the chaff…"

He looked at her beautiful hand, her masculine hand circling the air when she talked—that's the Italian in her. And her skin darker than skin. Her eyes greener than green eyes.

"But this is just… This is just honest, plain, brutal… Indifference... It's not like he's trying to protect his decision; he's not trying *not* to feel. This is just absolute, brutal, absence of feeling. Not even his sweater touched me when I leaned over for the jug. Even when I was exuding my energy, all of it, he was oblivious. God. I pulled so much. I pulled and I pulled, I kept pulling the finest, most invisible thread of fluff left between us. I said to

Sarah, loud so he could hear it, 'the cucumbers made the sandwiches soggy.'. Little things that should remind him of us, little winks to make him laugh, you know? But he's made of ice; he didn't pick up the extra cup I filled—he knew I filled it for him—he filled himself another one."

A space opened in her lungs, cold and huge like her front door opening, and Grant's things not being there. A void that opened under her feet. Like when he said, "I don't love you anymore."

Bryan's hand on her hand squeezed gently. She saw the Off-Licence just then, through the glass—and it felt like home for a second. Before pressing the buzzer like a cliff-hanger. Like her feet were dangling above infinity.

Press the loud buzzer again.

How many heads do I see?

Things I can count.

Things I can touch.

Two steps down.

My yellow Doc Martens on the pavement.

"I'll be ok," she said. "I'll stop talking about it when we get home."

"I know," said Bryan. He smiled a compassionate smile, but she only saw the man walking his dog. She only heard the door closing.

There was the building. She imagined her body plummeting from the balcony. Arms and legs twisted, like her mannequins. That would make a beautiful sculpture. Her heart beat loudly, ominously. Like the scary music in a movie as the key inserts into the keyhole. Except in real life she was still looking for the keys in her pocket. Bryan was looking at her young blue vein, at all the pain running through her beautiful young hand. Hands that made beautiful things. Fantastic things.

She clasped the doorframe. Archie won't bark—that's one thing she won't miss on her fabrics, his fur everywhere. But all the computers will be gone, his music. The closet. The empty closet. The emptiness will be there. The emptiness in her chest.

"I'm putting all my things in here," she said, looking at the spacious room. "My sewing machines. Everything."

She imagined her colourful paraphernalia piled up against the walls, but she felt sick underneath it all. Deep down, buried under every other truth, she wanted to do something wonderful for *him*. So that he heard of it. So that he admired her, wished he'd never left her.

She gripped the toilet seat. Veins ran swollen up her arms; her silent scream screaming for him to notice her, remember her, gushing out of her mouth like a torrent of doll parts.

She *will* wake him. The remnant of his love will surface somewhere in his subconsciousness. And she will rest her head in the sweet pillow of that certainty, because he has cut all ties, to the last thread, but true love doesn't die, and her art did speak to him once.

Or maybe love was just fluff brushing fluff. Maybe love was just fingerprints on fingerprints, kissing on plastic cups.

She looked in the mirror. Bryan was standing behind her. Her heart leapt; she hadn't *seen* him since he died—only *felt* his presence beside her since he stormed off from the solicitor's two weeks before his accident.

Grant hated her talking to Bryan. It was just too much for him, well over the line between quirkiness and madness. If he could only see Bryan now, gaining matter and particles, and flesh as she breathed—he would see her too; he would know she was right about him.

"I can leave now," he said.

Her hand rose silently to cover her mouth, like a scared doll; a bellow that didn't materialise and was sucked, instead, by the void of a dreadful door opening. Bryan had opened the door and found them, found her legs, her beautiful legs in a jumble of sheets, skin, and betrayal.

"I'm so sorry," she said, looking into his eyes in the glass.

"I know."

She hadn't meant to hurt him, but her joy of Grant was always far stronger than her sorrow. Not once did Bryan's pain cripple her. Not once did she *feel* it.

"I know you feel it."

The electrifying nearness of his body intensified. She longed to turn around and hug him, cry on the pillow of his chest. But what if, when she did, he wasn't there anymore?

She wanted goodbye to last forever.

First published, *Organic Ink Vol 1*, Dragon Soul Press, 2019

MOON SHADOW
By Kelly Matsuura

Prologue

Ueda Village. Koga, Japan

The sunlight faded from the sky. The

children, knowing they would be called home any minute, rushed to finish their game of hide and seek.

Reika, nine years old and the only girl in the woods, sat crouched behind an inkberry bush. Several boys were 'out' already, and sitting on a log chatting, but they couldn't see her. Shun, a boy the same age and her best friend, snuck over.

"Sshhh! They'll hear you!" she scolded him but was glad to have him close.

She took his hand and automatically rubbed the small scar on his palm with her thumb. She had an identical scar where they had pledged to be friends forever in blood.

"We're the last two!" he whispered.

Reika's brother, Tomoki, was searching for them. At eleven, he was the oldest in the group, and the one who always chose the games. Reika watched him and laughed.

"Oh, something just bit Tomoki's neck! He almost jumped out of his skin!"

She stopped laughing when she saw him stumble and fall to the ground, unconscious.

"Tomoki!" She ran to him, with Shun right behind. The other boys rushed to see what had happened. As they ran, they too fell to the ground.

"No!" Reika screamed as Shun fell beside her. She felt something sharp pierce her neck and her legs gave way. As she hit the ground, she saw several pairs of black boots edging towards them.

"Ninja..." she whispered as she drifted away.

Ten Years Later...

Yukiyama Village, Yamato, Japan

Reika knelt in front of the fire, waiting for Tomoki. She looked at the small wooden figurine in her hand and said a prayer. As Tomoki entered the room, she slipped the doll inside her obi. Tomoki sat beside her and poked at the fire.

She picked up another figurine wrapped in shiso leaves that gave off a pungent scent.

"Are you sure Yukio's dead?" Tomoki asked.

"Yes. There's no sign of him. My visions are blank. But the magic connecting us still lingers, so I must perform this spell." She began chanting and threw the figurine into the fire.

Tomoki didn't speak until she'd finished.

"So, the others are alright? Are they close?"

"Hiroji is weak, injured, but will recover. Daiye and Shun are well. They're camped on the other side of the mountain."

"Good. Red Moon and I will leave after dark." He glanced at the small lump the hidden doll made in her obi. "Shun won't remember you, you know that?"

"I know, but he'll recognise me from his dreams." Reika stared defiantly into the flames; they had been having this argument for years.

That day in the woods, they had woken up in the dark, and the four boys, who were like their brothers, were gone. The ninja must have thought Tomoki was too old for training and left him behind. They never took girls.

The families of the missing boys were heartbroken, and Tomoki and Reika were shunned by the townsfolk for being safe when their loved ones had been taken away forever.

Tomoki had begged to go and live with his grandmother in Shikoku, and his parents finally agreed, sending Reika as well. In Shikoku, a local wizard had discovered Reika's rare magical ability, and had taken her as a pupil. He found a master for Tomoki as well, a young man who had escaped the ninja order and had asked the wizard for protection. For years the siblings studied and trained hard, determined to find their friends. It had taken well over a year to catch up with Lord Oka and the ninja who were keeping Shun and the others.

Reika handed her brother a vial.

"Here, drink this. You'll sleep, and when you wake, you'll be strong enough to use magic tonight."

"Thanks. Be careful, won't you? The spell you are casting tonight is very dangerous. Don't reveal yourself too long." Reika was going to show herself in a vision to Lord Oka's mage; just long enough that they would locate her and send a ninja team out.

"Don't worry. They will think I'm a love-sick witch, searching for Yukio. Since he is dead, and I've destroyed our connection, it won't look so powerful." She smiled.

"Just...don't look at Shun. In the vision, I mean. They'll kill him if you do."

She nodded.

"I have a spell for that too."

"You have a spell for everything," he muttered as he drank the potion.

***

Moon Shadow lay under a tree, taking a nap before going on the night's mission.

In his sleep, he rubbed at the small scar on his hand, a habit he was unaware of.

He dreamed of the girl again; he caressed her face and kissed her warm lips and she looked back at him with love in her eyes. He called her Sunset, for the colours of her kimono. He had been dreaming of her for so long, a fantasy that was his only happiness in the wretched life he'd been given.

No one wanted to be a ninja; they were taken from their families at a young age and given a potion to forget their pasts. They were beaten and whipped for years, forced to train day and night. Fighting, always fighting. The boys who showed promise were taught to use magic tricks to confuse the enemy, but the training was dangerous, and so many boys were injured or burned. Some boys were killed before ever going on a mission, before becoming men.

Moon Shadow's dreams gave him the strength to get through anything. One day, he would be powerful enough to escape, and he would find Sunset. He truly believed she existed somewhere.

***

Reika joined her master in front of the altar. Everything was ready.

"Tomoki will wake soon. We should start your vision-walk," the wizard instructed.

Reika took the small bowl and pestle

she used for vision-making and selected the herbs she would need. She knelt by the fire and crushed the herbs while she recited the incantation. She sprinkled the enchanted herbs on the fire and fell into the trance that would allow her to visit the ninja's camp. She chose to show herself as a dragonfly because it was a hard form to take and would impress Lord's Oka's mage. In the vision, it was imperative that she didn't see any of the three boys she knew; it would endanger their lives. She had put the figurines that represented them into a small invisibility bag she had written the magic for herself.

This was her gift; most mage's learned magic from a skilled master, but only a few had the ability to create magic spells on their own. Reika wanted to show Lord Oka that she had the potential to create new spells, but that she wasn't aware of how powerful she could be.

She flew around the ninja's camp, pretending to look for Yukio. She put her whole heart into it, making the yellow body of the dragonfly glow brightly, ensuring she would be seen. She looked at the faces of the men in the camp, but thanks to her spell, she didn't recognise Shun or the other boys. She flitted around the campsite, examining each face but quickly moving on.

She left the camp and released the dragonfly form, showing her true appearance for mere seconds. She felt magic eyes on her as she dived into the tree hollow that would take her back to her body and end the vision-walk.

She opened her eyes, and her master handed her a cup of reviving tea.

"Well done, well done."

"Thank you, Master," she answered a little weakly.

The tea made her stronger, and she removed the figurines from the pouch. Then, she recited the invisibility spell backwards to reveal the three boys to her once more.

She held Shun's figurine and closed her eyes. The wizard turned away, pretending not to know what she was doing.

She found Shun sleeping and met him in the dream place she had created just for the two of them. When he arrived, he kissed her, and spoke words of love, but she didn't reply. She never spoke to him—he couldn't know she was real. She ended the dream and kissed the figurine.

"Tonight, my love, we'll meet tonight."

***

It was getting dark. Moon Shadow put on his boots and double-checked his weapons and magic pouches. Confident that he was prepared, he covered his head and face with a black scarf.

His best friend, Creeping Mist, came to join him fully dressed as well.

"Ready to go?" He stretched his

shoulders and wrists.

"I'm ready. Is it just us two?" Moon Shadow asked.

"No, we're going with three others to capture a witch. Another group is going into town to grab some boys." Creeping Mist's face fell. It was a task they all hated. Knowing it had happened to them once too only made it worse.

Most men were grateful that their memories of their childhood and families were erased after arriving at the training camp, but it was also heart-breaking to have no one in the world except each other. Moon Shadow and Creeping Mist had no way to know where they'd come from, but some instinct told them they had grown up together. There was an unspoken sense of love connecting them.

"Urgh, I hate taking boys, but I suspect it's a lot less dangerous than facing a witch. Do you know anything about her?" Moon Shadow asked as they walked to the edge of the woods.

"I heard she's young. And, she flew into the camp as a yellow dragonfly this afternoon. Did you see it? She flew right in front of my face. Amazing, don't you think?"

"That's incredible! Isn't a dragonfly one of the hardest forms to take? Most witches I've encountered change to crows or pigeons or something."

"Well, Black Morning said it's impossible to shift into an insect. He believes it was a type of mind-projection."

"Does such magic exist?" Moon Shadow had never heard of such a spell.

"I don't know." Creeping Mist checked the map in his hand. "Okay, this way. Let's go see if this young witch is beautiful. Maybe she's looking for a lover!"

***

Tomoki had left with his sensei, Red Moon. They would wait in the woods behind the house, watching for the five ninja they knew would come before midnight.

Their job was to make sure that only Shun and Daiye entered the house. They hoped to capture the other three ninja and offer them the chance to join their rebellion. If they refused, they would be left behind; their memories of the night erased.

"Are you sure we'll recognise the two boys?" Red Moon asked.

"Yes, Reika marked them with a yellow halo. I've seen them before from a distance," Tomoki explained.

"Ssh! Do you hear something?" They both listened to the sounds of the wind.

Three ninja flew into the clearing nearby; their black kites fell to the ground with barely a rustle. They didn't speak, only stashed the kites under a few bushes.

"They're not marked. Let's go!" Red Moon dropped from the tree with Tomoki straight behind him. It was a short fight:

one ninja leaped behind a tree, and flicked a few stars at Red Moon, who easily dodged them. Tomoki fought hand to fist with another and quickly overpowered him. The third ninja drew his katana and ran towards Red Moon; in three moves he was flat on the ground, his sword in Red Moon's hand. The first ninja stepped out into the clearing.

"You are...Red Moon? You're thought to be dead!" He held his sword in front of him but didn't attack.

"Yes, I am Red Moon. I am a free man. This is my apprentice, Tomoki. If the three of you wish to be free, you may join our rebellion. We do not want to kill you."

While Red Moon spoke, Tomoki placed magic cuffs on the three men, and chanted a spell to keep them confined in a circle.

"We'll keep you prisoner only until we find our friends. Where are Moon Shadow and Creeping Mist?" Tomoki asked.

"They cut through the woods on the other side of the house. They went for the witch. Is she with you as well?"

"She's my sister, and she can get us all away safely," Tomoki explained.

"Right. We should get Black Morning from the camp." Red Moon said to Tomoki.

He took two of the kites from the bushes.

"We'll just borrow these." He grinned at the bewildered prisoners.

***

LOCKDOWN PNR #1

Reika waited in the main room, knowing the boys were close. She held the two figurines tightly. For something to do while she waited, she knelt by the fire and placed a tortoiseshell over the flames. The cracks that appeared would show the near future. It was old crone's magic, but it comforted her to perform such a simple spell.

She closed her eyes and saw Shun and Daiye slip into the house through the side entrance. They were in black, of course, but she could see the soft yellow halo she had marked them with. She had marked all four boys with this magic many years ago, so she could always find them. It was another spell she had written herself and no one knew existed.

She sensed Shun in the next room and positioned herself clearly, so he would see her face when he entered the room. She took a breath to control her fluttering heart. They were so close now; she had waited for years, until it was safe for all of them. She was ready.

***

Moon Shadow went in first. As soon as he entered the house, he froze. He had closed his eyes for only a second, to adjust to the light, but he'd seen the garden from his dreams, and the girl, Sunset, smiling at him. Somehow, he knew she was here. What should he do? He had never told anyone about his dreams, and besides, it was forbidden to talk on missions. He used a few hand signals to indicate something was wrong, and he would take the lead. Creeping Mist nodded and stepped behind him.

Moon Shadow closed his eyes again and saw her clearly, sitting in a large room burning a tortoise shell on the fire. He touched the door in front of him; it was warm from the inside heat, and he knew she was there waiting.

He gave a final signal to Creeping Mist and opened the shoji door.

He stepped in the room, and the girl he knew as Sunset rose to greet them.

"Come in, both of you. I've waited so long to see you again." She held her hands out to Moon Shadow. Oh, she was so perfect! He wanted to kiss her and bury his face in her hair, but he couldn't in front of his friend. He did take her hands, though. How surreal it was to touch her at last.

"I am Reika. I know you don't remember me, but we all grew up together. I was there the day you were both taken, along with two other boys. We've been watching all four of you, my brother and I. Will you please let me show you who you really are?" she spoke gently.

"We can trust her. I…I know her." Moon Shadow pleaded with his friend.

"Prove that you know us. Who are the other two you speak of?" Creeping Mist looked at her warily.

"Your real name is Daiye. The other boys are named Yukio and Hiroji. You knew Yukio as Flying Fire. He died last week, protecting the rest of you. Hiroji is your friend, Black Morning. My brother has gone to rescue him now."

Reika looked at Moon Shadow.

"You, Moon Shadow. Your real name is Shun. We were best friends as children, and I've loved you my whole life." A tear slid down her cheek, but she smiled.

"I've always sensed…the four of us…" Creeping Mist couldn't finish.

"I'm so sorry about Flying Fire. We wanted to get you all out sooner, but we were too late."

Moon Shadow held her closer.

"Don't blame yourself. I can't believe you even found us."

Creeping Mist agreed.

"We've fought our whole lives. It's a miracle any of us are alive. I thank you for wanting to help us at all."

A brown owl flew in through the open door. In a blink, it shape-shifted into the old wizard.

"All is well here, I see. Tomoki and Red Moon are returning now with Black Morning, and three more ninja who've agreed to join us."

"Red Moon is here? I thought he was only a legend." Moon Shadow was impressed.

"He's here and will be the leader of the rebellion. We hope you'll want to stay with us and help recruit more men," The wizard said.

"Creeping Mist, let us go and meet the

other members outside; give these two a moment to talk." He gestured at the young couple.

"Yes, I'd like to see that Black Morning is alright, and I'm anxious to meet Red Moon." Creeping Mist said, smiling.

"Come along shortly. We all must leave before Lord Oka realises what we've done," the wizard told Reika and Moon Shadow.

"Of course, Master."

The wizard and Creeping Mist went outside.

Moon Shadow didn't waste any time kissing her.

"I knew you were real. You'll always be mine. We'll always be together," he whispered passionately.

He couldn't believe she was in his arms. And her voice! It was exactly as he had imagined all these years.

"My love, it will always be so," she promised.

First published, *Insignia Japanese Fantasy Stories*, BWWP Publishing, 2013

THE JEWEL
By D.J. Elton

She moans and screams. Groans and cries. Thrashing to the left, she howls and sighs. The baby will not come. Clutching her stomach, she lies in blood pooling below her, silk sheets bright red. Black blood. Royal blood. She dies, my beautiful wife, my Taz. The jewel of the night, jewel of the world. The mother of my twelve children, and this last one has caused her death.

I sigh and cry, hands tearing my hair, wanting to pull it out. I want to run my hands through her long black hair, loose, untied, at her knees. My beloved wife. She lays in a deepening pool of thick blood. Blood of the womb. No-one can help her survive. She has to die. It is foretold.

And what of I? I too die. Yet at night I roam the tomb, her tomb, and we meet again.

Every night we meet. I visit her tomb. I hear her whimpers and screams. She also now cries for the hundreds of men who died, hands severed in the creation of her tomb. Her death wail. Her agonised hopelessness clutches me and sends me on a morbid spin—a merry turn where I am mad in my heart for her, missing her, wishing her alive. No-one could help save her life as it went—a thin pale fibre. Air. Until nothing.

So we meet and I hold her, and she stumbles from her tomb to mine. For I am truly dead. She lays her long pale fingers on my arms, stroking the elaborate designs on the lid of her coffin. This mausoleum, which could be our palace, but no, instead a tomb.

Millions will adore the ceilings and the walls, such beauty, beheld as one of the most celebrated pieces of art and architecture ever known.

Then she falls, helpless, absorbed in my empty touch, as I hold her, hold us, together. We fade as morning falls. Into the pale, severe, golden light which is too bright, too alive. It colours our tomb as we float back to our caskets, forever together.

RESURRECTION
By Archit Joshi

"Strange," Paul Falcone mused. "You'd think the waves would've washed the body away by now."

His twin brother, Luca, noticed the

casket bobbing obstinately on a particularly turbulent sea but didn't remark. He was thinking about the note clasped in his palm.

Just then, the Don arrived in his Mercedes, the sudden revving purr of its engine making them jump.

"What's with the sea tonight?" Don Mickey Falcone walked with the usual jig in his step, which came from knowing not a soul in his town could lift a finger to him.

"I take it the job's done?" Mickey nodded at the casket. *That slimy bugger Roberto, knocking up my sister!*

His younger brothers nodded morosely. Mickey noticed their subdued demeanour.

"What's with you two? Did someone die here?" He went on to guffaw at his own joke.

"Mickey, Roberto left something strange behind before we did him in..." Luca produced the note in his hand.

Poring over the note, neither of them noticed the sea water slipping through the cracks in the casket. Nor did they hear the muffled thud with which the casket lid blew open.

"The bastard was trying to screw with your heads," Mickey roared. "You two should've stuffed the note into his nostrils before popping him." But deep inside, even the Don was a tad bit unsettled.

I'll be back, the note said.

A mountainous wave crashed at their feet, making them turn.

A wraithlike silhouette, formed of

effervescent water, hovered over the casket. The silhouette took on the shape of a person, its features slowly morphing into those of someone they knew.

"Rob...Roberto!" Paul gasped.

Before anybody could move, Roberto flew towards them and thrust his slippery, wet hands down the younger brothers' throats, choking their lungs with water, suffocating the air and life out of them. Mickey watched helplessly, unwilling to watch, but even more unable to tear his eyes away. His brain wanted him to run, but his feet wouldn't budge.

The ghoulish apparition of Roberto turned towards Mickey, sadistic rage outlining his face.

"I loved her."

Roberto leapt into the air and dived downwards, crashing onto Don Falcone's face.

The Don wheezed as icy water plummeted down his nostrils and gaping mouth. It felt like a fire burning down his insides, reaching his lungs and slowly devouring his heart. He desperately wanted to breathe, but the water, mixed with blood, left little room for air. The pungent, salty odour made his intestines retch, the vomit soon mingling with the rest of the racing water, finding the sinuses and the veins and the hollows in his skeletal frame, flowing under his skin, which was starting to lose its grasp on bone and flesh.

Convinced the bastard was deader than a deer hit by a speeding car, Roberto splattered on the seashore.

He lay stagnant on the sand for a thoughtful moment, then slithered towards the city, away from the sea, leaving three bodies in his squelchy wake.

Rosita, baby, I'm coming.

THE FIRST TASTE OF LOVE

By Galina Trefil

When first he had sauntered around, indicating his interest in her, she'd been intrigued. An introvert, she was very bulky and shy, but she enjoyed men that were cocky and small. This suited him, given he had the confidence of an 18-wheeler truck and was only half her size. She watched as, from a distance, his thin amber-hued limbs flexed and twisted seductively. No, he wasn't exactly dancing for her, but he *did* know how to shake it so that the ladies would pay attention. She tried to play it cool, but with each step closer towards her that he took, she found herself more and more on fire.

But even before the full relationship had formally begun, there were problems.

In the past, he'd bounced around, from lady to lady, crashing at their places until the love dissolved. This time, he wanted a more permanent home, he claimed.

Eventually, she came to realise that, rather than getting one of his own, his sights were set on *her* home. He moved in without asking; afterwards, he refused to leave. Older women might have known how to handle the situation, but she was still so young. This was the first time she'd been courted, and she wanted to make her much-cherished hottie happy.

From there, with each inch she gave, he took a plethora of miles. Everything that she had, she'd worked for, built with her own two hands, really. Artwork. Her trade, her profession. Her poem for the eyes in which she took so much pride. What had he done when he saw the masterpiece she had produced? Snip. Snip. *Snip!* He gave neither warning, nor explanation. He took the beauty she had crafted, not to mention the means through which she supported herself, and sliced it viciously to pieces.

She wanted to give him the benefit of the doubt. Maybe he didn't understand the gravity of his actions. Oh, well, she thought. She could always make more art. It would just take time to mend the damage that her beau had caused.

But every time she fixed it, he went right back to destroying it. She became furious, wanted to rip him in half! Didn't he understand how important her work was to her?

His haughty demeanour lacked any trace of apology. To the contrary, he didn't seem much concerned about her feelings on the matter at all. Perhaps, when a guy was that damn good-looking, he didn't have to care. He could do what he pleased and get away with it.

He played his sabotage off as simple jealousy. Her art was large and flashy. He didn't like the attention that it resulted in for her. Other suitors might see it, might be impressed, he feared. She was supposed to belong to him and him alone!

He was so controlling. Her patience with this destructive lay-about, squatter was running thin.

But then she saw that he was knitting her a gift. A bridal veil! Aw. Well, dang it. How could her ire, and her knees, not go weak now? Around and around, its gossamer, glimmering threads seemed to swirl and knot about her body. Never before had she felt so stunning and wanted. Yes, indeed, and that moment, she was his.

She surrendered to the romance, blissful and filled with anticipation.

Then it was over. Seriously? That was it? She scowled as he wandered off, sated and oblivious to her profound dissatisfaction.

Her house. Her life. Her livelihood. All destroyed and for what? So she could be fed some cheap promise of marriage from a ne'er-do-well? She took stock of what she had allowed to happen. No wonder he'd had to flee from the wrath of all of his previous girlfriends! No doubt, they'd been as frustrated and fed-up as she was.

She sensed right away that she was

pregnant. And, sure, he liked the idea that she'd carry his babies, enjoyed that she'd be bogged down by the added burden, which she knew he had no intention to help her out with. No, the only thing that mattered to him was that, so far as she was concerned, he'd gotten there first and, through her pregnancy, all the other guys would know it.

Things continued on like this for longer than she cared to admit. And her irritation continued to build.

Hormonal, hungry, and depressed, one day he pulled his crap one time too many. She would always look back on him, her handsome first love, with fondness, she assured him, but as he cowered in the corner, desperately looking for an escape route, her assurance was of little comfort. He didn't understand why she was so angry. What was wrong with women? Why did they always become so violent and irrational?

***

Oh well. Sooner or later, he scowled, as she bit ferociously into his throat, this was always the way it went. He could only remind himself as he perished that, inside of his massive and powerful ladylove, lay the nine hundred children conceived during their union. Those miniscule mouths cried out for the nourishment which he had denied to the mothers of his other spawn. Soon enough, 3600 little legs would be pitter-pattering all the stronger for the flesh which their father was providing.

***

Lazy bum, the black widow fumed, munching. He didn't even put up a decent fight! Ah, but she was not so hard-hearted as that. Indeed, to some degree, she was even sympathetic. Her dashing paramour hadn't done anything that both of their fathers hadn't, as well as their grandfathers, and so forth going back a hundred thousand generations.

Sadly, she knew that her next gentleman caller would likely treat her no better than her first had. Would she fall for his tricks too, allow more possessive buffoonery? Hopefully not.

But if she did, well, on a positive note, at least she had to admit one thing: this meal wasn't half bad.

THE MARKED
By R.A. Goli

Scarlett was being hunted. Separated from the others, she was running down a dark alleyway, skirting around discarded boxes and garbage. The creature leapt on her, knocking her to the ground. She bucked it off and rolled aside, leaping up and unhooking the scythe strapped to her back in one deft motion. She slashed the weapon at him as he circled her, but he parried easily, lunging forward. Quickly, she flipped the scythe around, stabbing at him with the handle, sharpened to a deadly point. She made contact, and the stake tore through his shirt and skin but missed his heart. He grabbed the handle and yanked it out of her hand, causing her to stumble forward. Close enough for her to smell his cologne. He grabbed a fistful of her hair and brought her neck to his mouth as she struggled to twist away. She felt her blood coursing through her body, the vein in her neck pulsing under his icy lips. He threw her against the wall and pressed his body against hers, his face only inches from her own.

"The slayers will kill you," she choked out, snaking a hand behind her waist. He grinned at her, tilting her head to the side.

"Perhaps, but not before I have fed on you." He licked her neck, sending a shiver down her spine—and not an unpleasant one. Aiden and Lucas had warned her about the vamps. They were seductive and could make a person believe it felt good, even when they were dying. She would not be fooled. She pulled the small dagger from her waistband and thrust it forward. His reflexes were too quick; he grasped her wrist, squeezing it until she dropped the knife. Her heart sank as she heard the metal clatter on the concrete, her last weapon.

"You could cooperate; it won't be unpleasant for you," he said, his dark eyes boring into hers, knowing her soul. She squeezed her eyes shut, not wanting him to charm her into submission. Flinching when she felt his mouth on hers, rather than turn her head, she parted her lips and let him kiss her. When he pulled away, Scarlett opened her eyes. He released her hair and clasped both of her wrists gently, holding them firmly at her sides. When he licked his lips, she saw the sharp white tips of his fangs and her heart began thumping wildly. She tilted her head to the side and closed her eyes.

The bite was exquisite. Just a hint of pain, the kind that was difficult to distinguish between ache and pleasure. She felt warm all over, as though her blood had risen in temperature by several degrees. Her womanhood seemed to throb dully, in time with his sucking, as if each mouthful of her blood were being drawn directly from that area. She moaned as he drank and was disappointed when she heard the shouts and heavy footfalls of her companions. The vamp pulled away and offered her a lopsided grin.

"That's alright. I've had enough, for now," he said, before running in the opposite direction. She watched his back as he disappeared around the corner.

***

Her footsteps echoed loudly as she headed into the red-light district. Capable of taking care of herself, she wasn't scared, but she hated the area. The place was scattered with vampire brothels and dealers, trading in blood and drugs, a mecca for miscreants. She ignored the undead men and women as they writhed, half naked in windows, beckoning her to come inside. When the laws were first passed that protected vampires, she had foreseen a different future. She feared the undead would take over the world and make humans their slaves. She was wrong. The fact they were outnumbered and forced to register were probably the main factors in preventing that outcome. Still, to see vampires prostituting themselves for fresh blood like heroin addicts repulsed her. They were a plague on society, and she had hated them for as long as she could remember.

She arrived to meet Aiden and Lucas at the Queen's Arms Hotel, a place notorious for being filled with vamps and the pathetic losers who worshipped them. She went straight to the bar and ordered a beer, then glanced around looking for her friends. They came here often; it was a perfect place for stalking their quarry. The two men were already seated and waved her over. She walked towards them. Halfway across the room, a vamp sidled up behind her. She rolled her eyes, but it wasn't unusual for one to approach a human in a place like this.

"Hello, Slayer," he whispered. She stiffened and turned. It was him. She stared wide-eyed as he circled her and then paused to move a strand of hair from her face. She tried to convince herself that the butterflies in her stomach were from fear, rather than excitement.

"I'm so glad you're here. Did you come looking for me, I wonder?" he said, his confident smirk both infuriating and arousing her.

"You'd better be careful," she said. "My friends are here."

"Oh, and what are they going to do? One word and you and your slayer friends would be surrounded," he said.

"You can't prove anything."

"Oh, no?" He stepped closer, his lips

near her ear. She felt his hand slide around her waist as he pulled her closer. His cool grasp felt comforting, and that frightened her. He tapped her dagger with a fingernail and whispered, "What about this?"

She stepped back, spilling some beer. "That's just for protection. Against creeps," she said, raising an eyebrow.

"Oh, I'm the creep?"

She looked passed him and saw her friends eyeing her curiously. "I need to go." She stepped around him and joined Aiden and Lucas at the table. For a brief moment, she wondered if she was protecting the vamp, or herself.

"What the hell was that about?" said Aiden.

"Nothing," she said, taking a seat. "He

just wanted to know if I was a donor."

"It looked like he knew you."

Scarlett sipped her beer, hoping the line of questioning would end.

"Why are you wearing a turtleneck?" Lucas asked as he reached out and tugged her collar down, exposing the bite. "You've been marked," he gasped.

"Fuck!" Aiden added. "We can't talk about this here, let's go."

***

"It's no big deal," she said, looking at each of them in turn. "I can handle it."

They were at the apartment they shared. Scarlet was seated on the sofa while Lucas and Aiden paced the floor.

"This is a big deal! You're marked. He'll come back for you," Aiden said, glaring at her. "You'll go soft. You won't be able to do your job properly."

"Of course I will. My feelings about vamps haven't changed."

"Sorry Scarlett, he's right. We can't trust you to have our backs," said Lucas.

"Either way, this can only mean trouble for us," Aiden said.

"How?" She protested. "How will this change anything?"

Aiden crouched down in front of her and smiled. He was handsome, and sometimes she wondered why they had never gotten together. But she knew why, really. He was not the type to let anything get in his way of killing vamps, and they weren't friends, really. Just three people thrown together by circumstance, and though she liked them both, each had kept their relationship professional. No-one wanted to get too close. The loss would be all the greater should one of them fall to the vamps.

"Okay, maybe you're right. The first thing we need to do is kill the vamp that did this to you," he said, watching her face carefully. She was unable to hide her discomfort at the thought. Lucas noticed it too and swore, running his hands through his hair.

"You see? He's already ruined you as a slayer." Aiden stood, shaking his head. "What a waste." He stormed off down the hall. Lucas smiled sympathetically.

"He'll calm down," he said. "But he is right. We need you on top of your game."

Aiden returned a few minutes later, his scythe strapped to his back. He looked at Lucas.

"Get ready, we're going hunting," he said. Scarlett stood, but Aiden placed his hand on her shoulder, pushing her back down.

"Not you. You're distracted, and probably still weakened from blood loss."

Scarlett was about to protest, but she saw the subtle shake of Lucas' head. He was right, she should let Aiden cool off; get rid of some of his aggression before they discussed the matter again. Ten minutes later, she heard the front door slam.

***

Scarlett lay in bed, running a finger over the bite mark on her neck. Though she felt physically exhausted from the loss of blood, she couldn't sleep. She kept her eyes fixed on the window and jumped at every shadow. Lucas and Aiden had offered to let her move in with them when they realised she was a slayer; for their mutual safety. Normally she wasn't uncomfortable being alone, but tonight she was on edge. A gust of wind caused the drapes to flap and she froze, only moving her eyes to scan the darkened room. She had shut and locked that window, as she did every night. Had she drifted off for a second?

"I know you're here," she called out, her voice sounding steadier than she felt. He stepped out of the shadows and approached the bed. She sat up, pulling the covers close to her chest.

"I could call the police," she said. "What you're doing is illegal."

Like a blur to her human eyes, he rushed to the bedside table and grabbed her mobile phone. She flinched and shifted away, uncomfortable with him being so close. He held the phone out to her.

"Go ahead," he said. "I shall be glad to tell them what you've been doing with *your* time."

She didn't take the phone, knowing the penalty for slaying was a lengthy jail term at best. Just like for murder.

"So, you've come to finish what you started?" She said, with only the slightest quiver in her voice. She hoped he wouldn't notice. He reached out a hand and stroked her neck, grinning slyly.

"Perhaps. Are you scared?" He said, shifting to sit on the bed. Scarlett swallowed, her mouth suddenly dry. Her heartbeat quickened, and she thought of her scythe under the bed. She would never get to it in time. The only other weapon was a hunting knife in her bedside table drawer. The table he was blocking. Though she always considered herself brave, her eyes brimmed, threatening to spill tears.

"Why are you upset, you seemed to enjoy it earlier?" He said sounding truly puzzled.

She looked up at him, frowning. "Because I don't want to die!"

He threw his head back, laughing

loudly. "That's what you think I'm here to do, kill you?"

"Well, aren't you?"

He laughed again. "Of course not, it's illegal."

"*Pffft*. So is feeding off people without permission."

He leaned closer; she could feel the cold radiate from his skin. "You didn't seem to mind," he said with a sexy grin. And it was sexy. Her stomach flipped and she squeezed her eyes shut.

"So, you're not here to kill me then. You've never killed a slayer before?"

"Oh, I have. I'm just not here to kill you. Not tonight anyway." He chuckled. She could feel him shift on the bed, but she resisted the urge to look at him. "Why are your eyes closed?"

"So, you can't mezz me like you did yesterday." Her mind kept replaying their first encounter, and how it had made her feel, though she tried to push the thoughts aside, she felt a stirring between her legs and her stomach did a flip.

"Mezz you…what the hell is that?"

"You know, use your vampire charm to make humans do what you want."

He laughed again and Scarlett risked a peek through half-closed lids. Again, he had thrown his head back and she could see his strong jaw line and the white points of his fangs. When he stopped laughing, she closed her eyes closed again. She felt his hand brush her face and she flinched.

"You can open your eyes. There's no

such thing as mezz or vampire charm. The only thing I used on you was my natural charisma and rugged good looks," he said. Slowly, she opened her eyes to see him grinning at her.

"You wanted it. You let me kiss you and you exposed your neck to me willingly."

She frowned, shaking her head. "No, that was…it can't be. I hate your kind," she said, unconvincingly. "And it felt…when you were feeding it felt…" She trailed off, not wanting to admit she enjoyed it.

"Well, it's a pleasurable experience. For both parties," he said with a wink, then grabbed the blanket that she clutched in her hands and drew it away from her. She opened her fingers, letting him, watching his eyes as the blanket slid down her body. He stopped when the covers reached her feet, and then slowly traced his fingers along the inside of her left leg. She shivered—in part from nerves, but also because his touch was cold on her warm skin. She swallowed hard.

"I'm not giving you permission to feed off me," she said, furrowing her brow.

He smiled, his fingers now at the top of her thigh.

"Are you sure?" His cockiness made her nervous. His hand moved from her leg to her neck, gently rubbing the bite mark.

"You're doing it again," she said. "You're mezzing me."

He chuckled. "I told you; there's no such thing. Just admit that I turn you on," he said. She watched his dark eyes and perfect lips in silence.

"Don't you find me attractive?"

"You're beautiful," she whispered. Then she leaned forward to meet his kiss.

A moment later his hands were all over her and she was tugging his t-shirt over his head. Time seemed to slow as they explored each other's body. There was no denying she was willing, when she once again tilted her head to expose her neck, inviting him to taste her.

***

The vamp flopped down beside her, smiling, and flung an arm across her stomach.

"What's your name, anyway?

"It's Reece. Yours?"

"Scarlett."

He made tight circles against her stomach with his fingertips as she lay there, catching her breath and staring at the ceiling.

"So, you hate vampires?"

She could hear the smirk in his voice even without seeing it. "Hmm," she muttered and closed her eyes, feeling drained.

"You can't hate us too much." He nuzzled her ear and her stomach fluttered.

She lay wrapped in his arms, her mind feeling like a lump of dough in a mixer. She had been taught to hate. The bedtime stories she had grown up with were rife with dangerous vamps, their existence a pestilence. Vile and unnatural, they were to be hunted and slaughtered, for the sake of humanity. It was all that she knew. And now, she had let one into her bed, let one feed off of her. And liked it. Now thoughts raced through her mind like a schoolgirl with a crush. She tried to push them aside, instead focusing on how comforting his cool arm felt lying across her stomach, and how he nuzzled into her neck, his hair tickling her cheek.

***

"Well, look what we have here," said Aiden, standing at the end of her bed, his scythe resting across his forearm. Alarmed at being woken in such a way, she grabbed her t-shirt and jeans, hastily dressing under the blankets. She saw that Lucas, his expression a strange combination of guilt and disappointment, had Reece cornered, his crossbow aimed at the creature's bare chest.

"It was a trap?" She said, hurt. "What if he killed me?" She shot a glance at Aiden who simply shrugged. "I was prepared to take that risk. Now you can watch your boyfriend die."

"Nooo," she cried.

Momentarily distracted by her shout, Lucas flinched, and Reece pounced. A flurry of movement. Then she heard the sickening crack of bone and Lucas's screams. He dropped to his knees, clutching his right arm. Reece snapped the crossbow and tossed the broken pieces at his feet. Then he swiped; the movement so fast it was like a blur. His sharp nails tore through Lucas' skin as though it were paper, opening his neck. Scarlett gagged when she saw the splatter of blood and chunks of flesh hit the wall. Then Lucas slumped forward, hitting the floor with a wet thud.

Aiden rushed the vamp, swiping his scythe. The vamp dodged, leaping out of the way as the weapon came down. Scarlett watched as Aiden chased Reece around the room, slashing at him and missing, but only by inches. Scarlett stared at the body on the floor, horrified, but also furious that they had used her as bait. She silently slipped out of bed and grabbed her own scythe. She saw Reece duck underneath Aiden's weapon, grabbing the handle and yanking it from his grasp. He tossed it like a javelin, and it became imbedded in the wall. Aiden pulled a gun from his waistband and shot Reece in the chest. The vamp staggered backwards, and Aiden shot him again, and again. Then the vamp leapt on him, hooking his claws into Aiden's shoulders as he sank his teeth into his neck and tore off a chunk of flesh. Aiden fell, landing heavily on his back, Reece still clinging to him. She watched, transfixed as the vamp drained him. Aiden's face contorted in a strange mix of agony and joy, before his eyes became still and empty.

Reece stood, wiping his mouth with

the back of his hand. It did little but smear the blood across his cheek. She saw the gun, still in Aiden's hand, resting on his stomach, where it had been pinned between their bodies. She pointed her scythe at Reece as she took a step backwards. The red welts where the bullets had hit him were already healing. He scooped his discarded t-shirt and jeans off the floor and put them on, pulled on his sneakers, and stepped towards her. Her hands shook, causing the weapon's tip to wobble. Her heartbeat sounded like galloping hooves in her ears.

"You going to kill me now?" she said.

He stepped forward and snatched the scythe easily from her grasp, tossing it aside. Scarlett flinched when it hit the floor.

"That depends," he said, smiling at her, though this time, the smile didn't reach his eyes. She took another step back until her bottom met the dresser.

He sliced the skin at his wrist with a long fingernail, then held the dripping arm out to her.

"The choice is yours."

She swallowed, trying to create some moisture in her dry mouth as she stared at his outstretched arm. His blood trickled to the underside of his wrist and dripped silently onto the rug. He said nothing as he watched her eyes darting from the dead men to his bloody offering. After what felt like a lifetime to her, but only a heartbeat to him, she inched forward, like a frightened bird investigating a discarded piece of bread on the lawn. Still as a statue, he watched as she cupped his forearm in her hands and curled her mouth around the wound. She took a small amount at first, crinkling her nose at the metallic taste, then drank more deeply as her body calmed and became accustomed to the flavour. When she was done, he kissed her bloodied lips, then went to the window.

"Good choice," he said.

Her heart pounded slowly but fiercely in her chest.

He grinned at her. "I was never going to kill you." He lifted the arm of his T-shirt to expose a birthmark on the underside of his upper arm. It was an odd mark, surprisingly intricate, almost like a circular rune symbol, but untidy looking, as though someone had spilled water over a painting. Exactly the same as hers. Her eyes travelled to her inner elbow, as though confirming hers was still there. When she looked up, Reece was gone.

Scarlett ran to the window, scanning the street and the rooftops, but she saw no sign of him. She wondered if he would come back for her, or if she needed to find him. It didn't matter; they were connected by blood now.

Looking at the bodies decorating her floor, she sighed. Any guilt she might have felt was gone. Far too tired to deal with them tonight, she covered the men with sheets, shut the window and drew the curtains. Stepping into the adjoining bathroom, she washed her face and saw that her reflection had already begun to dim. Steam from the tap fogged up the mirror, and she drew a love heart shape with her finger. She felt giddy. No longer a slayer; she had a new purpose. She wasn't clear on what it was exactly, she just understood it was with him.

Returning to the bedroom, she slipped off her jeans and climbed back into bed. She yawned and settled in for what she knew would be the last sleep she would ever have.

ETERNITY

By David Green

Ben looked into the mirror. He and Sophie bought it from a flea market, back when they'd first moved in together. The couple loved its simple beauty, its oval shape framed by silver flowers. Before leaving for work each day, they'd stand in front of it, taking a mental picture of each other, Sophie would say.

After she died, Ben couldn't bring himself to stare into their mirror. Their apartment didn't seem like home anymore. Sophie had been there one day and gone the next. She'd tripped when crossing the road, a thing people did without thinking.

For weeks, Ben stopped living. The dirt and grime building up in the apartment, his hair greasy and facial hair dishevelled. His friends' phone calls ignored, and their knocks on the door unanswered.

Until he found her.

Ben didn't know how, but Sophie hadn't left him. Not really. He woke one afternoon, his sleep pattern having turned from regular to staying awake until he passed out from drinking too much or exhaustion. Whispering woke him, snatches of words on the edges of his hearing. Ben followed the noise until he felt certain where it came from.

The mirror.

He'd covered it with a sheet at some point. With a shaking hand he reached out, exposing the glass. Shocked, Ben looked away from his own reflection. He hadn't realised how much he'd abused himself. The whites of his eyes red, the bags under his eyes almost purple. Pimples and angry red sores blemished his face.

With a shudder, he looked again. The whispering had stopped. In the reflection, by his shoulder, was Sophie. She didn't speak, only looked at him with her sad, brown eyes. Sophie smiled as tears rolled down her face.

From that day, Ben looked after himself. He didn't want Sophie seeing him the way he'd let himself become. He showered and shaved every day, wore clean clothes. Ben would stand in front of the mirror and tell Sophie about his day, his thoughts and what they'd be doing together if she'd still been there.

Sophie didn't always appear, and he couldn't figure out why. Ben returned to the flea market they bought the mirror from, but the stall had closed down. None of the other workers remembered the woman who worked the stand.

Determined, Ben scoured the internet, looking for any stories he could find about enchanted mirrors, convinced that the mirror held magical properties. He realised he was desperate and never believed in such things, but couldn't argue with what his eyes told him.

At last, he discovered what he searched for. Ben and Sophie would reunite the next full moon.

Surrounded by a circle of lit candles in front of the mirror, Ben smiled at Sophie, her reflection still sad. He'd dressed in the clothes she liked best on him, had taken extra care when shaving and showering. He'd even flossed twice.

"I told you I'd be with you forever," he whispered, "and I've found a way. Do you trust me?"

Sophie gazed back, love in her chocolate eyes.

"We'll be together soon," he said.

He raised the kitchen knife he held with a tight grip and ran the edge down the palm of his hand. Ben winced as the skin tore, blood running down his wrist. He pressed it against the glass, below Sophie's reflection.

"Now for the next bit," he said with a ragged breath. *I can do this.*

Ben stared into Sophie's eyes and smiled as he pressed the knife against his throat.

"I love you," he whispered, drawing the sharp edge across his soft skin.

LOCKDOWN PNR #1

***

"The apartment comes unfurnished," the estate agent said, waving with disregard towards a mirror with silver flowers mounted on the wall. "Except for that old thing. Won't come down for some reason, though it has its charm."

Daneen glanced at the mirror and smiled. She liked it. The whole apartment appeared too wonderful to be true. A perfect location, spacious and affordable. She'd Googled the place and seen the previous owner had committed suicide there after his girlfriend had died in a freak accident.

Cranks on the internet spoke of the place being haunted, and that's what made the rent so low, but that didn't bother her, Daneen wasn't the superstitious type.

The estate agent left the room, and Daneen followed until something caught her eye as the sunlight struck the silver rim of the mirror. She moved towards it in disbelief. Reflected in the glass stood a man and woman, foreheads touching, staring into each other's eyes.

"Hey!" Daneen shouted, hoping the estate agent could hear her. She turned away, looking for the woman.

When she returned her stare to the glass, the couple had vanished. Daneen let out a breath and chuckled.

"Got myself all worked up over ghost stories," she said, moving away to explore the rest of the apartment, hoping her boyfriend loved the place as much as she did. He'd told her they'd be together forever, and this felt like a perfect place to call home.

CLEAVING
By Dawn DeBraal

Long after my friends had given up on their "starter marriages," Frank and I still cleaved to one another. Yes, I said cleave, as in the Biblical "cleaving," to stay with one another. No matter how mad I could get at Frank or how disillusioned I became, I still loved him. Most of our friends had moved onto other relationships. We were the constant in the storm. How odd that the word cleave means both binding and severing? How is that possible? We just refused to quit. No one is better than my spouse, we both said. Frank and I watched the carnage of our friend's relationships fall apart. We remained standing strong.

I continued to grow older. Frank remained the same, retaining his boyish charm, the bastard. He told me every day I was beautiful. He told me he loved me too much to make me suffer what he had suffered, as a creature of the night.

I could go out during the day shopping

and do what I pleased, while Frank was stuck indoors, down in the basement. Sunlight was his enemy. He needed a front, and I was his person, but I was also his wife. Our friends didn't think it weird we could only get together after nightfall. They thought Frank's business dictated it. When the plans didn't fall in line, I went early, telling our friends Frank was working late and would be by later on. They never put two and two together. Frank took to putting silver in his hair. It made him look dashing. But he didn't age. No amount of make-up would make him look as old as me, which frustrated me to no end. Frank said he didn't care, but I cared. How could such a good-looking man be cleaved to an older woman?

It wasn't always that way. Frank was quite a bit older than me when we first met. I was eighteen, and he was twenty-eight. Now that I was forty-eight and he was still twenty-eight, the difference showed.

I begged him every day to change me. He said the life of a vampire was miserable. Seeking blood from humans was a repulsive act, and living had become an exercise in duration. It drove him crazy. He longed for the old ways in a world that kept changing. I wondered how many wives Frank had before me.

We would need to move soon. Our friends were getting suspicious as to why Frank looked so young, and I didn't. The house sold quickly. We moved across the country, so former friends did not feel inclined to look us up. We purchased a beautiful home online, with a little property to go with, giving us some privacy.

At dusk, I pulled over to the side of the road, opening the trunk. Unzipping the body bag, Frank came out, kissing me deeply, then slipped into the passenger seat. We made it to the house. The moving van had been there the day before, and many of our things, packed in boxes, would require most of the night to put away. Frank sct up the coffin in the basement—a root cellar without windows—then helped set the bed and unpack many boxes. Before dawn, he kissed me and retired. I went to bed too.

The next evening, the doorbell rang. I answered, wondering who would call so late. It was the neighbour with a hot dish for supper.

"I knew you'd be unpacking today, so I've brought a casserole."

"Oh, thank you." I took the dish and she walked in behind me. Startled, I told her the place was a mess.

"My name is Myrna. I live next door." I heard Frank coming out of the basement. He strode across the house, extending his hand.

"Hello, I'm Frank Cape, and this is my…mother…Vivian." My mouth fell. His *mother*?

Myrna shook both of our hands and then said she would leave us to settle in.

"Your mother?"

"I am sorry, my dear, it is getting

harder to pass ourselves off as husband and wife. We still are, of course, but that would make our story more believable to our new neighbours. It is why we moved, remember?

Frank was extra nice to me that evening. A bottle of wine, candlelight…with the curtains drawn, of course. We talked well into the night. I went to bed, and Frank did what Frank does until dawn.

When I woke, I felt the loss of my husband. I was going to have to act the part of his mother in public, and that didn't sit well with me. It was during my second cup of coffee that it hit me; I didn't need to be Frank's mother when I could be Frank's widow!

Down into the root cellar I went, allowing the daylight from the basement windows to come into the darkroom. I opened the coffin where Frank rested, allowing sunlight to pour over him.

His eyes flew open. He tried to grab me, but as I stepped away, the full light of the morning sun hit him, searing his flesh. I took the wooden stake I'd brought with me and drove it through his chest. Frank shrieked and burned in front of my very eyes.

It was over. We were cleaved.

The doorbell rang. Myrna again. I opened the door, hoping I didn't look too dishevelled from the murder I had just committed.

"Good morning, Vivian. I was

wondering if I could talk to your son. He seemed like such a nice young man. I wanted him to meet my daughter, Tammy."

"I'm sorry," I told her. "Frank left early this morning. He went back to Baltimore. He was just helping me move into my new home. He is so busy with his work. I'm afraid he won't be back any time soon."

"Such a shame. I thought Frank and Tammy would have been perfect for one another. I smell something burning…is everything all right?"

"I wanted to bake Frank some muffins to take with him. It's that new stove. I've always had an electric range, not gas. Poor Frank only got burnt offerings for breakfast. Would you like a cup of coffee?"

Myrna was more than happy to accept my invitation and fill me in on the neighbourhood gossip.

RAINFOREST REVERIES

By Zoey Xolton

The explorer stood transfixed, his gaze firmly locked upon the pale green woman standing alongside the waterfall. She was lithe and comely, with long, clover coloured hair, her modesty maintained only by the living, writhing vines that snaked their way around her glistening form.

"Will you join me in my lagoon?" she beckoned, her voice plaintive and soft.

Mesmerised by her beauty and allure, he waded into the sparkling waters.

The nymph joined him, and their bodies entwined. Cupping his face, she pressed her lips to his, and the young man sighed…forgetting everything and everyone, but his ethereal rainforest fairy.

THE FAREWELL

By Christopher T. Dabrowski
Translated By Julia Mraczny

It's time to say goodbye. They don't want to part but have no choice. Force majeure.

When they look into each other's eyes, all the memories come to life. Like a film on a mental screen. They knew each other so well, and experienced so much, that they became one. The unity of souls and bodies. They read each other's thoughts. Hugging one last time, tears come to their eyes.

What comes next? Will they still be together? Will they meet again?

They aren't afraid of death. Only that it' ll separate them.

They evaporate immediately...absorbed by the atomic bomb.

DRESDEN DOLL
By Hari Navarro

One day, on my way to school, I happened across the body of a newborn baby bird. I thought it badly made—as I thumbed the cold flesh that hung too loose, it slid atop its fragile frame of barely formed bones. It was a sensation I was to feel again; the kiss of bloodless skin as it writhed in near-freezing embrace against mine.

I felt it yesterday.

No, what am I saying? It was last week, or last year, or never. Maybe it never happened. Maybe none of this happened. Maybe I never happened.

But it did. I know I am here. I have to exist, for if I didn't, then neither would you, and you have to be here. You, who are everything.

"Can you hear that? That clink, clank, that scraping tap..."

Mother collected dolls. She called me her little Dresden doll, and I guess my pale face and sullen pout did echo those things she most treasured; those damned, accursed, porcelain creeps. Bloody things used to scare me half to death, as they seemed to move beneath the lick of the candlelight flicker. She used to ask me what would become of us if we were ever to be scared half to death twice. Mother thought she was funny; even when she hit me, she laughed. Mother also collected pain.

"…the tapping sign. That metal plate attached to its pole... No, it isn't a pole, it's a tree. That's right, it's a sign wired to a tree. And it hangs and it taps, and it taps and it taps, upon the wire that holds it just so. The wire that attaches it only just—for it is so old and worn and rusted—to the pole. Sorry…the tree. A sign with a word…*Dresden*…though I can only just see the Dres…"

We are so toxic in death. This new death. This un-death into which we have been infected. Some of us, at least. Those of us chosen by the good lord to stride ever onward past the last beat of our hearts. Dead, but long dormant instincts revive, and we grope for the ladder…we rot, yet we pull ourselves towards the light. We, the chosen.

"…I hear the slip of the chain as you pump your beautiful legs into the pedals…"

The ladder…the twisted helix that animates our corpses so as to drag us back to the exact place of our births. The instinct that pulls. Back, always back.

Back home.

"…and you pant, and you bite the thick roll puff of your lip, and the pollen catches like gentle, lost stars in your hair…"

We are abominable weapons. At first we were mourned, and then, when we started to come back, we were feared. And then came the war, and we became ordnance. The perfect spore dispersion system… We that will rot the Reich from the outside to the in and have it fall away into this nightmare of living death.

"…I watch as you stand high astride the saddle and your dress pulls tight at the small of your back…"

***

Can you see the glow? Over.

I can see three target indicators through cloud. Over.

Good work. Can you see the reds yet? Over.

Can just see reds. Over.

Plate Rack, Plate Rack... OK boys, come in and bomb glow of red target indicators... Dresden is hot... Bomb doors open!

Bombardier...

Steady... Steady...

***

Dresden. The infernal place. The rusted, tapping sign. The word itself, such a truly wicked torment. I remember correcting her, correcting Mother. They are Parian Dolls… No such creature as a Dresden Doll, I said. That day, she ruined my voice.

The doors opened. We fell. There was a kind of lull as the air pummelled in throbbing waves and ripped the stink up and away from the poor scabbed pores of our flesh.

"…I hear you sing, though it's only ever a hum, through the humid stick of your lips…"

Fire. Ever folding blankets of seething orange. Roaring heat and I sink down into the furnace mist, and I smell my hair as it melts.

People trample and fall and ignite and

flare. A man, with his face burnt away, clutches a photo in a frame. Buildings hollowed as gales of flame run as liquid. We that were dead. We who fell from the sky. We that are smashed and burnt, we stand and our bones crunch as their ruined shards mash and the contamination splits and spits from our skin.

I believe we accomplished our mission. We who created a swath of our plague clean through the belly of the enemy as we dragged our bones back to dear England. I will never know for sure, but I am convinced that the Nazis will fester and fail. They have to, right? Or else, all this waste was for nothing.

Fire does terrible things to the body… It contracts… It compacts and the doomed fuse together and children contort to the size of…dolls… I happened across a wicker basket with a baby inside… A loved thing hurriedly staved beneath wet sheets…and still now my body fills with the greasy steam scent of its death.

"…I love you…"

I collapsed and grappled, like a clicking slug, across the charred earth until the meat rolled from my fingers. I ripped the bones from the waste of my legs and used them as stakes, thrusting them into the dirt before me and pulling myself to this place.

To this peace. To you, my beautiful love, and your badly oiled bicycle and the tree with a sign that taps.

"…Blood beads at the graze on your

knee. What shame as I look upon you, unasked, hidden from you, wedged down in this pit, this drain, hooked tight beneath the bramble and sucked into the mud at my waist. But, as I watch you now just mere feet from my gaze, please know this to be true. Know that I am happy and I am complete. I am dead and yet have never once felt so alive. And I deny the noose of my instinct, and I forget about my home, and I forget about my mother, and all I can think of is you."

First published at 365tomorrows.com, 2019

SAME TIME NEXT YEAR

By J.W Garrett

I stroll the beach, grateful that the past six months have been a hazy blur. My husband's death from a car accident brought me to my knees, and I still haven't totally re-entered society.

Those first few days had been excruciating, even making it from one moment to the next. Paralyzed by grief, time had become my obsession, while the days eked painfully by.

As the weeks pass, I stumble through the routines of getting back to work and people. But I see life differently now, through a lens tinted grey. Somehow that makes going on a little easier, muting the colour of my days that used to be vibrant and happy. For now, dreary, lifeless, and a little out of focus match my psyche perfectly.

Today would have been our three year anniversary, and it seems stupid now, but I keep the reservations that Kyle made for us over a year ago at the beachfront property in Nags Head, North Carolina. We were married here and vowed to return each year to celebrate.

I hold the gift that Kyle probably got for me the same time he made the reservations. And I smile inwardly, since I'm pretty sure I know what it is. As I watch the sun sink lower along the horizon, my eyes close, and I let the warmth seep into me, little by little easing into the desolation of my heart, still shut down tight.

Dropping into a chair on the porch with a glass of wine, I tug at the glittery silver paper. My lips turn up in an action that seems foreign and out of place, but the book has the intended effect. I revisit our tentative decision to have a baby after three years of marriage. Through my smile, tears escape, sliding down one by one.

Brushing them away, I suck in a breath and steel myself, determined to see this through. My hands slide across the cover of *Where the Wild Things Are*, and on the first page I read, *Vanessa, are you ready?* with the question mark taking up half the page. A half laugh, half sob escapes me. I am…but of course, it'll never be. His few words tear a hole inside me that I have no idea how to heal. Below his handwriting, an envelope clings to the page. I lift it free.

Let's take a walk just after sunset, and you can give me your answer then. I hesitate, glancing at the sky, because what does it matter at this point? But the sun, just barely there, calls me forth like a beacon, and driven to comply, I gulp the last of my wine, scoot my feet into sandals, and head to the beach.

The sun sets as a cool breeze washes over me. One hand holds my shoes, the other the book, and I set out to nowhere in particular. With each step my feet disappear into the wet sand, plastering the tiny grains to my feet and ankles. Darkness falls, its cover cloaking me in an invisibility that I welcome. I scan the shore where cottages dot the beach with little flares of light. How far should I go? Surely I've fulfilled this last request of his.

Turning toward the waves spilling forward, then retreating, I whisper my response. *Yes!*

The winds shift, and the tide rises higher, angry, as it thrusts water, shells, and sand on the shore, spraying me and burying my feet with its wrath. In the mist forming in its wake, a shape emerges.

I step backward, tossing a glance to my left and right, then squint, looking straight ahead again, not sure I'm really seeing this. I'm dreaming—I must be. Drops of water mingle with the low light, twisting, turning. Held together by the sea and sand, a vision of Kyle steps forward and offers me his hand.

I can't find the will to care what others may think because, somehow, he's found me. Real or not, my husband stands before me. I reach for him, and where our hands connect, my skin meshes with his, fading into a construct of light and water just like his. Where we're joined, my body tingles. A smile eases up his mouth, and I take another step; he meets me, our bodies flush against one another.

My form matches his now, and as our bodies writhe and spiral, he lowers his mouth to mine in a kiss that reaches inward into the depths of me, breathing a different kind of life through this new shape I inhabit.

He lets go of one hand and nods to the beach, where my book and shoes still lay. Instinctively, I understand that I can return. Instead, wanting more, I wrap both arms around his neck, while the mist fully engulfs us both and our bodies sway, a soft whisper inside the night.

I give one last glance to the book as it washes out to sea, but I don't linger because, nestled next to Kyle, I envision our future stretching out ahead of me.

COME FLY WITH ME
By R.J. Meldrum

It was the first week of September when I heard the news. A casual comment made by my mother during our weekly phone call.

"Oh, David, I forgot to mention. Lucinda Collins died last week. You knew her, didn't you?"

For a moment, my breath choked in my throat. Lucinda…dead. I hadn't thought of her for years. Her name sparked a flood of memories in my mind.

***

Collinswood. That's where I grew up. We learnt in school that the Collins family, the ones who lived in the big house on the hill, were the family who originally founded and named the town. It had been Joshua Collins, steel magnate, who established the steel mill on the bank on the Avon River in 1858, just in time for the outbreak of the civil war. The war made him rich. Rich enough to expand his mill, rich enough to build houses, schools and libraries for his workers. Rich enough to name this new town in his own name.

By the time I was born, the Collins no longer owned the steel mill. It had been sold to a huge corporation in the 1970s. Before that, the operation had been failing, as falling steel prices drove the plant towards bankruptcy. The prosperity of the town depended on the mill. My father worked there, so our family depended on it too. Just before the banks foreclosed, the corporation arrived, saving the town from disaster. The sale of the mill made the Collins even richer.

Lucinda was the younger of the two

daughters of Arthur Collins, grandson of Joshua. She was about two years older than me. I didn't really know her; the Collins children didn't attend the local high school; instead they went to a boarding school in the city. We, the locals, only saw them during the summer break when they returned to town. We didn't know them; we didn't approach them. They were different.

If this was fiction, rather than real life, I would tell you I first met Lucinda by rescuing her from the town bully or by saving her from drowning in the local swimming hole. The truth is far more mundane. I met her for the first time when I was fifteen, at the end of August, just as we were about to return to class. I was wandering by myself, as I often did, in the hills above town, near to the Collins house. I wasn't a lonely kid, but I was introverted, content with my own company.

She was standing on the hill, flying a kite. The warm summer wind held it aloft and with delicate flicks of her wrist, she made it dance across the blue sky.

I stood, transfixed. She eventually noticed me.

"So, David Williams, are you just going to stand there with your mouth open, collecting flies, or do you want to have a go?"

Embarrassed, I walked over. She handed me the cord that held the kite.

"You know my name."

"I know everyone. It's my father's town."

There wasn't much to say to that. She stared up at the sky.

"I love flying kites, it takes me away from my life. My family, my school. It gives me the freedom I seek."

I'd never heard anyone speak like that before.

"Summer is still here, but it's about to say farewell, once again. Fall is nearly here, you can feel it… The mornings are colder; the leaves are starting to change. This is the time of year when you can still see the light, but you know the darkness is coming. Change is on its way."

I stood quietly, unable to respond. I was fifteen, a baby.

***

I fell in love with her that day. During the years that followed, I always remembered her words. I started to notice the big changes in my life occurred just at the point when August yielded to September. The point in the year when the darkness began to subsume the light. I started my undergraduate studies in September, the same with my graduate work. I started my academic career in September. I got married at the beginning of September. I got divorced in September. I lost my dad in the same month. Everything big in my life happened at the beginning of September. Every time something happened, I thought of Lucinda.

And no, I didn't marry Lucinda. I wanted to, believe me, but it wasn't to be.

After our first meeting, we only saw each other sporadically. As I grew older, our paths separated. She had her friends at the posh school, or at the country club. She didn't mix with the townies. My friends couldn't understand why I smiled and waved at her when I saw her. Why I would run over to say hi. Eventually, their mocking made me self-conscious, made me stop. Lucinda looked hurt when I ignored her. She didn't understand I had to make a choice. Hang with my buddies, who shared my background, or mix with the Collins, the snobs who were too stuck-up to speak to the locals. I was a kid; the choice was obvious.

***

LOCKDOWN PNR #1

I moved away when I was eighteen, off to the city to study at university. I was the first in my family. For a few years I lost sight of Lucinda; I rarely returned home and our paths never crossed. New friends, a girlfriend and the pressure of studying made me focus on places and people not related to Collinswood. My mom kept me up-to-date with the gossip, so I was vaguely aware of what was happening. Lucinda finished high school but didn't go to university. Instead, she returned to the big house on the hill. The townsfolk, my mother included, expected her to marry well, produce a couple of babies, then spend the rest of her life moving between cocktail parties, lunches, and spa days with her rich, spoiled friends. She didn't.

I was enrolled at grad school, and my visits home became even rarer than before. My mother mentioned Lucinda during one of our phone conversations. She was the talk of the town. Lucinda was becoming a recluse, hardly ever seen in public. The only time she was seen was when she flew her kite on the hill where I first spoke to her. That news caused a thump in my chest. Eventually, my mother stopped mentioning her. The townsfolk had moved onto more interesting gossip. Lucinda became the eccentric lady who lived on the hill. There were other things to talk about. The town forgot about her. I forgot about her.

***

It took my mother's phone call to bring all the memories flooding back.

"Yes, Mom, I knew her."

"She was only fifty-three."

That would be correct, she was two years older than me.

"They say it was cancer. Her parents died years ago, she lived in that big old house all by herself, locked away from the world."

"Did she still fly her kite?"

"She did, crazy lady. Everyone laughed at her. She should have known better, an adult playing with a kid's toy."

I smiled at the memory of the day I'd met her.

"When's the funeral?"

"Third of September. Are you thinking

of coming?"

"I can get someone to teach my first week. Yes, I'd like to come home, pay my respects."

"Well, it's been so long since you came back. I suppose I'll have to make do with you deciding to come home for her, and not me."

Mum sounded pissed. I guess I could have chosen my words better.

"I know I don't come home as often as I should and I'm sorry, but Lucinda was a friend. I want to say goodbye to her."

"I'll see you soon, David. Love you."

* * *

After the funeral, I climbed the hill.

The Collins house lay empty. I stood staring at it, lost in a haze of memories and regret. I wished I'd done something about Lucinda. I saw a kite flying, just over the brow of the hill. I walked towards it. It was her, standing as she had, all those years ago.

"So, David Williams, you finally came back."

"I did. To say goodbye."

"I'm glad, thank you."

She took her eyes off the kite for a second to look at me.

"I know you loved me; I know you thought about marrying me, but you do know our families would never have agreed. We would never have been content. Can you imagine the family get-togethers?

Our parents wanted you to marry some mousy, drab thing from your own social class and so you did. My parents wanted me to marry into money, like my sister did, to consolidate the Collins wealth and status. Instead, I flew my kite. It was a better life."

She glanced at the sky.

"The darkness is coming again; can you feel it? This is the last time I'll see it, but I won't miss it. I'm going to a place where there is no darkness."

She stared at me.

"I will miss you, David. Here, take my kite. Remember me."

She passed the cord over to me. For the first and last time, our fingers touched. Then, without another word, she simply faded away, leaving me alone on the hillside. I stood there for a moment, thinking about life, love, death, and the passage of time. It took a moment for me to realise I now had another reason to remember this time of year.

HUSH
By Stacey Jaine McIntosh

Dirt and wet leaves tangled in my hair as he pushed me to the ground. He pressed his hand over my mouth and whispered. "Hush or they'll hear you?"

I struggled against him. His body was warm against my own, making me shiver. My damp gown clung to me uncomfortably. It took all of my willpower to stop myself from curling into his side in an effort to stay warm.

All too quickly, he removed his hand from my mouth. "They're gone."

I peered out into the darkness. I hadn't seen or heard anyone. It was hard to imagine hearing anything over the sound of the rain. I couldn't help but think he had made the whole thing up to get close to me.

Ever since we'd first met, Prince Marsden had wanted me for himself. Even going as far as to beg me to marry him instead of his brother, Riordan. I had to admit; I was tempted.

But queens weren't allowed to rule with their hearts. We had to rule with our heads instead. And my head told me Prince Riordan was the wiser choice.

Prince Marsden had too much of a reputation. He used and discarded women far too quickly and according to his brother Riordan, he'd left a string of broken hearts all throughout the Winter Court. As a knight, his life was devoted to keeping the king and queen safe. But now the Winter Queen was dead, and the king wasn't much of a king because of it.

I got to my feet, brushing dead leaves and dirt from the skirt of my gown.

"Why are you helping me?" I hissed, keeping my voice low.

"Rumours are rife throughout the

Winter Court," he said. "Word is they want you dead. I find myself woefully tired of politics. Life as a knight is boring when there aren't any damsels in need of saving, and you, your highness, are no damsel. Although I fear you might need saving."

"Charming as always," I murmured. "Sir Marsden."

"You are awfully formal for one who is no longer afforded airs."

"You forget, Sir Marsden, I never wanted to be queen. I was quite content with my human life before I even found out the queen of the Summer Fey was my mother. She can resume her duties with my blessing any time she likes."

He smiled and grabbed both of my hands in his. "Run away with me!"

"Runaway with you?" I asked.

"You could run away with me. Detroit is a far cry from the opulence of Faerie, but no one would find us there. Not even your betrothed."

"Riordan? Oh, he'd be devastated."

"No, he wouldn't," Marsden said. "He was only ever using you for your title. My mother and grandmother were all using you. They wanted the crown, and they didn't care how they got it."

"I..."

"Say yes, Saoirse, please?" He dropped to his knees before me, still clutching my hands in his.

How could I say no when he was begging me to say yes?

I simply couldn't.

So, I did the only thing I could do. I said, "Yes."

BABA YAGA MAKES A HOME

By McKenzie Richardson

Baba Yaga lived alone. She ate children for dinner, they said. But before that, long before, there was a time when

Baba Yaga had not been alone.

***

Viveca quietly crept down the dirt path that led into the forest. The night was dark and cold, but the stars gleamed with a fierce light that matched the burning in her heart.

She stepped up to the door of the little house sheltered in the midnight shadows of the trees. The silent clearing exploded with noise when her dry knuckles met the door's hard surface.

In an instant, Dinara's face appeared in the crack of the opening portal. The initial worry that aged her features gave way to relief when she recognised Viveca's outline in the darkness.

"You came," she gasped, a smile spreading across her face.

"Of course."

The two women embraced, then disappeared inside the little house.

"They say you are a witch," Viveca said as they sat by the fire in each other's arms.

"Do *you* think I am?"

Viveca rested her chin on Dinara's bony shoulder. "I think it doesn't matter. I think I love you."

It was the first time those words had been spoken aloud in this way.

Dinara smiled. "I think I love you, too."

They spent the night lost in each other's eyes.

***

But the thing about unbridled happiness is that it doesn't last forever. Humans have a way of destroying all that is beautiful.

One night, as lips explored skin, there was a banging at the door.

Ice shot up their spines as frightened eyes met in the dimness.

The banging continued and soon harsh words infiltrated their haven.

With a burst of splinters, the door was kicked in, angry voices and rough hands emerging through its broken frame.

Viveca and Dinara were yanked from the house, their words useless against minds that did not understand, did not want to understand.

When they reached the village, twin stakes stood waiting, kindling stacked at each base.

They were tied to the matching poles, their white slips glowing in the darkness like a pair of stars preparing for their lights to go out.

A man advanced with a torch, not meeting their eyes. The flame flickered as their crimes were read and punishment determined.

Suddenly, a great burst of wind swept through the village. It whipped hats from heads, tore shingles from homes, and extinguished the flame of the hovering torch.

Dinara disentangled herself from the ropes that bound her as though they were strands of yarn. Once freed, she outstretched a hand in Viveca's direction, clenched it hard into a fist, and the bindings fell away.

Frightened villagers fled the scene, but others too consumed with hate to admit defeat brandished impromptu weapons with grim determination.

A torch lashed out at Dinara, but she didn't even blink. With a sweeping movement, she took hold of the flame, snatched it right from the top of the torch, plunging the rest of the world into darkness. The man who held the now-dead torch stared dumbfounded for a moment before sputtering backward, retreating into the line of startled eyes.

In her outstretched palm, Dinara held the dancing fire, which cast wicked-looking shadows across her once-soft features. Then she blew into her hand and the flame erupted into a wall of fire that encircled her and Viveca, cutting them off from the harsh shouts of the terrified villagers.

She turned to Viveca, desperation in her eyes. From the pocket of her apron, she pulled two small objects and placed them on the ground. She held her hands over them, palms down, and the objects began to grow. Soon, Viveca could make out a mortar as tall as her waist and a pestle the size of a broom.

Then Dinara was beside her. The

angry voices behind the flames raged against their ears, beckoning water to be fetched. Dinara led Viveca to the mortar and guided her inside, then handed her the pestle.

"Take this. Use it to steer." Dinara looked deep into Viveca's eyes. "One day, I will find you again." She pressed a hard kiss to Viveca's lips, one that spoke of love and sorrow too powerful for words to describe.

Then, she lifted the mortar as easily as a stone and threw it up into the sky.

As she floated away, Viveca never took her eyes from the glowing circle, Dinara at its centre slowly disappearing from view. A heaviness filled Viveca's chest, but the mortar flew on, cold to her loss as it took her deeper into the darkness of the night.

***

Years passed and Viveca aged. Sorrow can do that to a person.

She went back to the house in the woods, so full of reminders of what was now gone. With time, the house sprouted legs and wandered the earth, always searching for its missing occupant. Some days Viveca took to the sky in her mortar, watching all that occurred below. But she always came back to the little house, hoping her lost love would find it again.

You never can tell just how much pain a heart can hold. It's always more than you think.

Baba Yaga lives alone in the woods, remembering a time when she was not alone.

FOUR DAYS IN AN ITALIAN VILLAGE
By P.A. O'Neil

Tuesday

"Please, won't someone help me!" The old woman leaned out of the upstairs window, her breasts pushing over the plants in the ceramic pots on the miniscule balcony as she strained to attract a passer-by.

It was mid-morning and the narrow streets of the quiet Italian village were empty. It really did not matter though, as the street was as empty as it had been the morning and evening before.

"There's no use in crying out, Signora Rizzuto, there's nobody coming." The voice was that of a woman, below the window but out of sight. "You heard the *poliziotti*, yesterday when they drove through the streets, 'By order of the *Magistrato*, shelter in place.' None of us can leave our homes. If we need food, a van will make its rounds to see that food is left at the door."

"But you don't understand, Signora San Filippo, it's my husband, my Carlo, he is terribly sick, he needs a *medico*." But there was no answer from the landlady downstairs, as she had already turned away from her open window.

"Lara, Lara…" the raspy voice from behind her called her back into the small flat. Lying on the old double bed, her husband of almost forty years. His arms reach out before him.

"Carlo, you shouldn't try to get up." She felt his feverous brow as she tried to press him back onto the pillows. "Let me get you a fresh cloth." She picked up the wet rag, now warm from the transfer of the heat from his head.

Signor Rizzuto raised his chin, tilting

his head back, and began coughing. Each spasm shook his upper body so that his chest would raise off the bed and throw him back so violently, he barely had time to recover before the next would lift him again.

Signora Rizzuto returned with the rag, now saturated with cool water, just in time to catch him from slipping off the bed, as he had turned, trying not to choke on the phlegm clogging his throat. She wiped his mouth, readjusted him on his pillows, and then refolded the rag before placing it on his forehead.

"Pray for me, *amore mio*, I haven't long to live." His voice was weak, and every few words were prefaced with a gasp for breath as he strained to speak.

"Oh, Carlo, you don't need prayer, you need help."

As her husband seemed to quiet down, the sound of a motor driving away pulled her attention back to the window. "No, no, no! Come back, please!" A white van with the crest of the town magistrate was already down the street and turning the corner. Signora Rizzuto pulled herself back in from the window, her shoulders sagged as she leaned against the shutter.

"Signora Rizzuto, Signora Rizzuto…" A knocking came from her front door. She looked at her husband who lay still, breath laboured, and moaning. Running to the door, she opened it to find her landlady, Signora San Filippo, back against the opposite wall, a mask covering her face.

"I collected a box of food for you and your husband. It's not much, just some wine and bread and cheese. They said it should last a couple of days."

She looked down at the cardboard box at her feet.

"Thank you, that was kind of you. Did you tell them my husband was sick? When will they be back?"

Signora San Filippo backed away, placing more distance between her boarder and herself. "They said everyone was to stay inside. I don't know if they'll be back tomorrow." Her last words trailed off as she turned down the stairs, no longer wanting to talk.

Signora Rizzuto watched the woman flee, then looked down at the box. She whispered her thanks and bent down to bring in food she did not feel like eating.

Wednesday

"*Agente di polizia…*" Signora Rizzuto furiously waived a red scarf while she yelled, hoping to catch the attention of the young officer on the other side of the street.

"Signora, we must remain calm," he yelled back as he crossed the street to stand under her balcony.

"Signor, my husband, my Carlo, he has died. Please, I need someone to come and take his body to be buried."

The officer was taken aback by the woman's request. He looked down and shook his head. He signed and looked back up. "I'm sorry, signora, but the Magistrato says we are to follow the *nazionale* guidelines for prevention of the plague. No one is to leave their *domicilio*, and if there is a death, the body must remain for no less than two days until the chance of *infezione* has passed."

Signora Rizzuto placed her hands on her cheeks. "No, no, I cannot stay with a dead body for two days. Please, you have to help me."

"Signora, it is beyond my control. I will report the death and return in two days to claim the body of your husband, until then, do you have enough food?" Signora Rizzuto nodded her reply, too numb to speak. She lifted one hand to acknowledge his departure.

Downstairs, Signora San Filippo,

nodded to the policeman as he caught sight of her before he turned to leave. She shuddered, crossed herself and closed the door.

Thursday

Signore Rizzuto sat by the open window overlooking the street. It was the middle of the night, but no one would know she was there as the room was dark.

After the policeman left, she had sat in her kitchen for hours, looking at the shell that had been her husband. *Two days. After two days the body will begin to corrupt*, she thought. She spent the rest of the day cleaning up the remnants of his illness. She washed the rags she had bathed him with and sterilised the basin that had received his discharge.

Finally, she pulled out his old blue suit, and with the newly cleaned rags and basin, she stripped his body and with the tenderness of a new mother, bathed and dressed his dead body in preparation for anticipated burial. She combed his greying hair and draped a light blanket over his body. After washing the rags and basin a second time, she returned to her bedroom, and kneeling along the far side of the bed, began to pray her rosary.

That had been several hours ago and now she sat in the dark, occasionally looking at the night sky, or admiring the way the moonlight played off the flowers she had forgotten to water—anyplace but back into the bedroom at the draped figure laying where her husband used to sleep.

"Thank you for preparing my body, *amore mio*, you didn't have to do that."

The voice was male and recognisable, although absent was the gasping for breath, the strain to speak without coughing.

Signora Rizzuto never took her eyes off the twinkle of the heavens. "I did it for myself as much as for you, anything to help put off the stench of decay."

"Really, Lara, 'stench of decay', now where is the romance in that?"

Signora Rizzuto turned her head with a measured stillness, into the bedroom at the visage of her dead husband, only not dead, grey hair combed and dressed in his blue suit. Her eyes looked past the man standing by her side of the bed, to verify there was still a form under the blanket. "Two days living with a dead man, I'm sure is never pleasant, so excuse me if my choice of words offends you."

"Now, *amore mio*, is that any way to talk to your husband?"

"My dead husband?"

"Dead, yes, but still your husband. Did we not take vows together; 'in sickness and in health, etcetera'?"

"Yes, we did." Signora Rizzuto raised herself off the floor to speak face to face with the phantasm. "But the vows were ended with 'till death do us part'."

The man smiled and gave a small snicker. "You always were the pragmatist, Lara."

"What is it you want, Carlo? Why

haven't you moved on?"

"I'm lonely, Lara, come with me. We can be together for eternity."

Signora Rizzuto tilted her head down and closed her eyes. She took a deep breath of rapidly fouling air and looked up at him, pointing her finger as she spoke. "No, Carlo, no! For almost forty years, I have lived by your side, and now another two days by your death. I must say no, I choose to live."

Friday

"Oh, thank you for coming. The smell is becoming more than I can live with."

Signora San Filippo opened her door to a police officer and two associates in white coveralls, all wearing masks.

"Yes, signora, are you the woman with the dead husband?"

"No, no, that is Signora Rizzuto, she lives upstairs. It's Signor Rizzuto who passed away. If you'll come with me." With a dish rag covering her nose and mouth, she led them up the stairwell to the neighbour's flat.

The policeman knocked on the door. No answer. He knocked one more time. "Signora Rizzuto, it's the Polizia, we've come for Signor Rizzuto." There was still no answer, not even the sound of anyone coming to the door.

"Signora…"

She lowered the dishrag. "San Filippo."

"Si, Signora San Filippo, do you have

a key to this flat?"

"Si, si, I'll go get it…"

"Never mind, it's unlocked. Please stay out here, signora."

Taking all caution, he opened the door to the small flat only to be met with the beginnings of putrefaction and the sound of a motor from the street below coming through the open bedroom window. The three men looked between the four small rooms; the only evidence of recent inhabitants was a cardboard box of unopened food on the kitchen table. In the bedroom, the policeman lifted the blanket off the face of the corpse. "Call that woman in but stay close in case she faints."

Signora San Filippo, escorted by one of the men in the white suits, peeked in from the kitchen, not daring to cross the threshold to the death room.

"Signora, do you know this man?" He raised the drape again but lowered it as soon as she began to nod.

"Si, that is my neighbour, Carlo Rizzuto, but where is his wife?"

"You tell me. Did you hear her leave the house against orders?"

The woman shook her head in rapid succession. "No, no, the only exit is past my door, and I would've heard her, even at night. I am a light sleeper. She has to be here."

"Take Signora San Filippo downstairs and come back up." When she had gone, the policeman signalled for the other man to check the wardrobe, while he went to the window. He stood looking down at the street, remembering where he had stood when he spoke with the woman.

"This is full of clothing, both male and female. You don't think she jumped out the window, do you?"

"No, a woman of her age wouldn't have made the jump. Besides, the plants haven't been disturbed—you would expect that, if she crawled out this small balcony, they would've been tipped over." He joined the other two men. "Bag this man and take him to the van."

"Aren't we going to go looking for his wife?"

"What for?"

"Well, she might've killed him?"

"An old woman might have killed her

husband, tells the world he is dead, only to be told she has to remain alone with his body for two days. No, I'd say she has suffered enough. Besides, we've other places to be."

CLOSING TIME
By Raven Corinn Carluk

I clicked off the last of the lights and made a final round to double-check the locks. Elysium was my bar, my baby, and I was protective of it. Even a month after opening, I still did everything with a mix of nervousness and pride.

How long until running my own haven became second nature?

I paused near the private stairs to draw a deep breath of the mixed scents. Human and Other and lust and alcohol. Comforting and familiar, while also completely new and different. Master's haven had never smelled quite like this, even if he'd run his bar exactly as I was now running mine.

A wave of hunger rolled from my core, nipping at my nerves, setting my fangs to aching. I groaned, clutching at the doorjamb, struggling to stay on my feet. Far too long since I'd hunted, and I hadn't moved a Font in yet. Too much time spent being a manager and a business owner, and not enough time spent being a vampire.

I hadn't learned all of Master's

lessons, apparently.

The moment passed, leaving me gasping and shaking. Only a few hours until dawn. Still time to hunt, to find human prey. But no guarantee that it would be good blood, and it could only be quick and dirty, no enjoyment for either of us involved.

It would have to do. I couldn't go another night without feeding. A century of unlife gave me *some* endurance, but not enough to run this ragged this long.

Now that I'd acknowledged it, the hunger dogged every step. Not a frenzy, no lack of control, but a constant, driving, painful urge. Bordering onto compulsion. I practically raced up the stairs to my apartment, wanting to at least change into clothes I wouldn't mind getting dirty if things got out of hand.

I burst into my apartment, pulling my hair from its topknot, then realised the door had been unlocked. I stopped and sniffed the air, seeking the intruders, claws extending. Someone would be sorry they'd broken in.

But I didn't smell intruder. This was a mingling of sweat and Irish whisky, smoke and cologne, elf and human. Familiar and new and wild and strange.

"I didn't mean to startle you," Aubrey said, stepping from one of the shadows. My half-elven barback-sometimes-waiter with the smile that made all the female clientele swoon, red hair down and shirt open across his pale chest, a tumbler of amber liquid in his left hand. "I just thought—

"What are you doing in here?" I interrupted, too sharp, too fast. My fangs ached as hunger lashed through me, Aubrey's very male, very delectable scent filling my nostrils. My feet remained planted on the floor, thankfully. If I moved, I would attack the man in front of me.

One dark red brow quirked briefly, then he gave me his winsome smile, eyes sparkling. "I was certain you needed a drink." Aubrey lifted the glass for a slow sip, tongue playing across his lips after he swallowed.

Gooseflesh prickled sharply across my skin. I couldn't look away from him, couldn't keep my eyes off the play of muscles as he took a step closer. "You know I don't…" My voice trailed off as I attempted to fight off the heat rising through my core.

He nodded slowly, taking a second step with bare feet. He'd made himself quite comfortable in the hour since his shift ended. What else had he been doing while waiting for me? "You made it very clear that you were a vampire when you hired me." Another sip of whisky, another dance of tongue across his lips, another step closer to me.

Holding my gaze with emerald eyes, Aubrey pushed aside his shirt and touched a line of scars along his chest. "You wouldn't be the first one I've worked for. Just the first one that didn't already have a Font."

I sighed. Maybe even moaned. I was losing control, couldn't tell exactly what noises I made. "You need to leave," I choked out, unable to look away. The ache in my fangs spread into my jaws, made my vision blur. His scent grew stronger, and it wouldn't be long before I lost my fight with the hunger.

Aubrey shook his head, draining the rest of his glass before dropping it to the rug. He moved again, his shirt falling from long arms. "Do I *really* need to leave?" The half-elf stopped just outside arm's length and cocked his head, giving me the slightest of frowns.

His scent wrapped around me, warm and spicy and sweet and desirous. I groaned, nearly a growl, and barely kept still. "Yes. You do." I might still be learning how to manage a haven, but Master had insisted that I never feed on the employees, nor hunt my patrons. As tempting as the half-naked man in front of me might be, I couldn't give in, couldn't break that rule.

Aubrey pouted, lowering his eyes. "Would you really send me away like this?" He unbuttoned his pants, pushing them down an inch to reveal black silk underwear.

I couldn't fight the temptation any longer. Not with an invitation like that.

A growl escaped my lips as I closed the gap, pulling him into a fierce kiss, hunger cracking through me like a whip. He sighed, opening his mouth to my probing tongue, and wrapped his arms around my back. I clenched a fist in Aubrey's silken hair as I pressed the length of our bodies together, and he pulled us toward my couch.

We tumbled back in a tangle of limbs, need blinding me to everything but the play of flesh and heated skin. My hands drifted across his shoulders and his strong chest, my fangs pricking his lower lip. Aubrey's hands squeezed at my thighs and hips before drifting under my shirt along my back.

His fingers burned on my scalp as Aubrey took a handful of my hair, breaking the kiss. I moaned, scratching at his shoulders before moving my mouth towards his neck. "Please," he begged breathlessly, writhing beneath me. "Take me."

Time paused as his plea goaded the beast inside. A small tremble started in my limbs, made its way to my core, where it became a raging force that tore apart all sense of self. I was a creature of instinct now, driven only by base desires.

With a snarl, I drove my fangs deep into Aubrey's tender neck.

He groaned, long and deep, the sound reverberating through my chest, and clutched tightly to me, arching up against my body. Aubrey's heat blasted across my skin, his scent suddenly full of the deep musk of lust. Blood filled my mouth, and I was lost to the feed.

I tasted and heard and felt Aubrey's

heart as it pounded against my fangs. Strong and young and powerful, pumping the delicious richness of his blood into my mouth. I swallowed, then groaned, then bit deeper.

Never before had I tasted anything like this. Master had cautioned me about Others, warned that their blood could be more powerful and more intoxicating than humans. It could become easy to be lost in their essence, to feed too long, and fall into a fugue, taking the partners too close to death. It could become a need, an addiction, and one that might never be fully sated.

Aubrey was all that and more.

He was a contrast of flavours and sensations. Light and dark, sweet and coppery, rich and airy, filling and never-ending. The thickest elixir that had ever crossed my lips, but the softest wine upon my palette. Nothing I'd ever had before, but the culmination of every taste I'd learned.

I tried to savour the moment, tried to experience every nuance of the way we moved together, of how his skin felt beneath my lips, of how I grew heated with every swallow, but I couldn't focus. I couldn't think. I could only *be*. Could only feed.

Aubrey gave a short cry, weakening beneath me. His hand fell from the back of my head, and his heart skipped a beat. Even the flavour of his blood changed.

I was old enough, with enough control,

to come back from the edge when my partner had given all they safely could. Taking one final, deep swallow of his essence, I pulled back, groaning in appreciation. His scent followed me, tantalizing, and I had to sit up, straddling his lap, lest I sink fangs back into his neck.

He sighed when I leaned down to flick up a drop of blood with the tip of my tongue before pulling away again.

We stroked each other, remaining close, recovering from the intensity of our intimacy. I traced scars and muscles with my fingertips, smiling every time he jumped or writhed. Aubrey caressed and squeezed my thighs and hips, his breath ragged and lined with moans.

After some unknown amount of time,

Aubrey brought one of my hands to his lips, kissing each fingertip before speaking my name. I opened my eyes to his stunning smile, though it faded quickly, and his eyes barely glittered beneath mostly closed lids. "I'd like you…to consider my application," he managed, voice hardly more than a whisper.

I frowned, licking the flavour of him from my swollen lips. "For what?"

He sighed, closing his eyes completely, growing more slack beneath me. "To be your Font. To do this…whenever you need."

I leaned down to kiss him softly on the corner of his mouth. "Consider yourself promoted."

LET ME GO
By Stephanie Scissom

"I can't sleep," she whispered as she crawled into bed and spooned against my back.

"Jesus, you're cold," I murmured.

She snuggled closer, throwing her leg

over mine. I lay there for a few beats, caught between my alcohol-induced sleep and wakefulness, until I realised whatever this cold thing pressed against my back was, it was not Danae. She'd been in the grave three months now.

My eyes flew open, but I couldn't move. Adrenaline surged through me, but I lay paralyzed except for my eyes and my thundering heart. The icy thing holding me never moved. Instead of it taking on my heat, I took on its chill.

I fought against it, and somehow managed to wiggle my toes. Then my whole body spasmed, pitching me out of bed onto the floor.

The crack of my face against the hardwood dazzled me and filled my mouth with blood. I struggled onto all fours, terrified I'd find some dead, exsanguinated version of Danae peering over the mattress at me.

A glance at the clock dispelled some of my terror. I couldn't be late again. Even though I half-expected an icy hand to cover mine, I grabbed the mattress and pulled myself to my feet.

The empty bed held a tangle of sheets and pillows, but no dead, accusing wife. I didn't shower, or even brush my teeth. I threw on my uniform and ran out the door. This job was all I had now, and I sure as hell wasn't in any shape to find a new one.

At the hospital, I swung my truck into the Emergency Department parking area and ran inside. I clocked in with twenty-eight seconds to spare.

Tony, my night shift partner, frowned when I burst into the Security Office. "Dude, you look like shit."

I glanced down at my half-tucked shirt and rumpled pants. I hadn't even brushed my hair.

"I'm sorry. I haven't been able to sleep, and when I finally did, I crashed."

He stood and motioned me to follow. Like a chastened toddler, I did. We ended up in the family restroom on the first floor. Tony ducked out while I washed my face with pink liquid soap and dried it with paper towels. He reappeared in a moment with a plastic tub that contained a toothbrush, toothpaste, comb and deodorant.

"I'm worried about you," he said.

My mother, my brothers, and Abi all worried. Looking at my red eyes and drawn face in the mirror—hell, even *I* worried about me.

"I can't sleep. And when I do, it's nightmares."

"Do you take anything? Melatonin, Ambien?"

"Does whiskey count?"

He didn't smile. "Jake, we're all real sorry about Danae. We loved her. We love you. But you gotta pull it together, man."

I nodded, and he left me alone to make myself presentable. When I came out a few minutes later, Tony was gone. I grabbed my clipboard to make my checks.

Hospital security wasn't a bad gig. On

the weekend, a lot of the areas were empty. Of course, tonight's full moon would probably have the psych ward hopping.

By the time I'd done my first walk through, I felt better. I wandered down to the Emergency Department waiting room. Twice a day, local churches brought in meals for the families in these waiting areas. I nodded at the volunteers, filled a Styrofoam plate with food, and then stepped outside.

Mack grinned when he saw me and stubbed out his cigarette before reaching for the plate. "It's the Baptists tonight, ain't it?" he asked. "Those little women are the best cooks."

I laughed. "Yup. Fried chicken. Want me to ask any of those little women if they're single?"

"Shoot, no, son. Papa is a rolling stone."

We chatted, then I told him I needed to head back in. As always, he thanked me. Technically, we weren't supposed to feed the homeless, but we all loved Mack. I wasn't about to let a decorated war veteran sit out here hungry when a table creaked with food inside.

Walking back through Emergency, I saw Abi turning the corner and hurried to catch up. I tugged her ponytail and she turned to smile at me.

"Hey, Favourite," she said. "What's up?"

She'd called me that as long as I could remember. We'd grown up next door to each other. My three brothers, at some point or another, had all competed for her attention. I was the Favourite, however, or as she liked to tease them—#1 Fults. The others would alternate being #2 and #3, except for Joe, who annoyed her so much he was always #4, or she'd tell him he was her least favourite Fults. Even as adults, Abi and I still lived next door to each other. She'd helped me get this job, and also tipped me off to the house I lived in now.

"Not much," I said. "Seems quiet so far."

"Shh!" she admonished. "They'll hear you."

I'd probably opened the gates of Hell just by uttering that. To say a night was easy always seemed to curse it. We walked to the elevator and the doors opened before I could even press the button. We looked at each other.

"Abracadabra!" I said, motioning her inside.

"So, how are you?" she asked.

"I'm good."

"Liar."

"Good enough, then," I said.

"You did all you could do."

"I wish people would stop saying that!" I snapped, before I could stop myself.

She punched the fourth floor button and I sighed.

"I'm sorry. I failed her, Abs. We were fighting and I just drove off."

"There's no way you could've

known," she insisted.

"I told her I wanted a divorce."

Abi's eyes widened. "You never told me that. How come you never told me that?"

The elevator doors dinged open. Abi dragged me to the staff break room. She pushed me into a chair and said, "Talk." When I didn't speak, she said, "Halverson?"

The hospital had buzzed with rumours of an affair. I hadn't told Abi when Danae finally confessed, because that would've destroyed any fragment of friendship they had left. I didn't suppose it mattered now.

"Halverson was part of it. She admitted it."

Abi shook her head, eyes narrowed.

"Again? She cheated on you again? With *Halverson*?"

Abi's disgust at Halverson's name stung a little, because she didn't know the worst of it. Not only had Danae slept with the old doctor, she had done it for a price.

"She confessed and begged me to forgive her. That wasn't even our real issue. She was back on the pills again. Halverson wrote her the script."

Abi gasped. "You should turn him in! He knew her history. He should lose his license."

"I can't prove he knew."

"I never really believed the rumours about them. I even asked her point blank one day. She denied it, and I believed her. I'm so sorry, Jake."

It wasn't the affair that bothered me most. Danae said that it was just sex, and I believed her. She could shut herself off in ways that I didn't understand. At times, I was closer to her than anyone, but there were places in her heart where even I was a stranger.

Abi and Danae had gotten along well enough, but I never doubted where Abi's loyalty lay. Danae had always been jealous of her, but I'd made it clear from the start that my friendship with Abi was non-negotiable. I'd never been unfaithful, never given Danae a reason to doubt me. She couldn't say the same.

"We fought again that day. I'd come home and found her high. I told her I wouldn't live with someone I couldn't trust, so I got in my truck and left."

Danae had chased me into the yard, crying and begging me to stay, but I'd jumped in my truck and roared off. She tried to call me a dozen times, then I got that text. By the time I made it back home, it was almost too late. Hell, I guess it had been too late, because she'd never regained consciousness. I got lost in that memory, of busting down the bathroom door. Of her pale face sinking in that swirling red water.

Abi squeezed my hand. "Stop. It wasn't your fault. Danae had a history of depression. She tried to kill herself the first time long before she started working here. Long before she ever met you."

"That's why I should've been more careful. I saw one attempt, remember? I knew how fragile she was."

"You didn't know she'd do that. You are not God."

My pager buzzed and for once, I was grateful. "Gotta go. Transport."

"Okay," she said. "But swing back around later. I love you, Favourite."

"Love you, too, Abs."

The worst part of my job was definitely the transports. Carla, the nursing supervisor, waited for me in the ER.

"Hey, good lookin'," she said. "Ready to take a ride?"

I liked Carla. She was good at her job and strong as an ox. If I had to do a transport with anyone, I'd just as soon it be her. But I grimaced when she led me to exam room #3—the room they'd wheeled

Danae to when we first arrived.

Thankfully, a sheet already covered the body. "Is it a child?" I asked.

"Naw, she's in her twenties. A tiny thing."

We transferred the body from the bed to the gurney, then took the staff elevators to the basement. Carla and I made small talk, then she left, her job completed. I pulled up the computer screen, opened the morgue book, and moved the sheet to look at the dead girl's toe tag. The tattoo on her foot stopped me cold.

A daisy.

Danae had one in the same spot, gotten on our first date. I'd taken her to a little hole-in-the-wall bar to see my favourite band, Goodbye June. She'd fallen in love with their song "Daisy" and I'd fallen in love with her. Daisy had evolved into my pet name for her.

Though I knew the girl on the slab wasn't her, that the tattoo wasn't even the same, it spooked me. Tendrils of this afternoon's nightmare brushed me, threatened to wrap around me again. I forced it from my mind and hurried to complete the computer work so I could leave.

Her cell phone blared to life with 3 Doors Down's "Let Me Go," and I jumped backwards, banging my head on a shelf. It would've been funny if Carla had still been here, but in my current state, it scared the shit out of me. The song blasted on as I scribbled my entry in the morgue notebook.

I didn't know how her phone even had a signal down here. That's why I carried a pager.

Only when the door closed behind me did I feel like I could breathe again, but my relief was short-lived. When I approached the elevators, the doors opened again without me getting near the button. I almost didn't have the nerve to get in. Things had been happening around me for a while now. Creepy things. Objects moved around the house, phone calls with no caller information, her songs on the radio. I didn't know whether to attribute it to too much alcohol, too little sleep, or losing my damn mind. But any of those things were better than the alternative that Danae was haunting me.

The next few hours passed uneventfully. At midnight, I went to find Abi for lunch. She looked up when the elevator doors opened. I waved and headed toward her. As I walked past one of the rooms, a sound from inside distracted me. Beep, beep, beep in a frantic rhythm, like someone's heart thumping about 170 beats per minute. It sounded so odd that I stopped to listen. It slowed until it was more like beep...beep...beep. Then it stopped altogether.

"Hey!" I yelled. "Someone's coding."

Abi gave me a confused look but didn't move.

"Hurry!" I shouted and threw open the door.

An old man sitting up in his hospital

bed glowered at me, then turned his attention back to *The Price is Right*. The noise—the beeps—someone had just spun the fucking wheel.

Abi appeared at my shoulder. She snickered, then burst out laughing.

Feeling really stupid and trying not to smile, I shut the door and muttered, "Asshole."

Abi laughed harder, until she had to lean against the wall.

"Code Bob!" she squeaked, and I laughed too.

"It's Code Drew now. Come on, jerk, and I'll buy you lunch."

She grabbed her purse and we headed to the cafeteria. I told her about the girl in the morgue, thinking I'd get another laugh, but she squeezed my forearm and said, "I'm sorry."

I didn't want to talk about bad things with her. She had been there for me enough. She'd been working Emergency the night I'd carried Danae's dripping, almost lifeless body through the doors, screaming for help. After trying to tourniquet the mangled wrist she'd slashed so deep and vertically, I'd panicked and thrown her in my truck. We lived so close to the hospital I thought it would be faster than waiting for an ambulance. Abi told me that had been the right reaction, although it hadn't made much difference.

The cafeteria didn't have much selection. I grabbed a cheeseburger and Abi got a plastic-wrapped salad. When she reached for it, her sleeve pulled up, revealing the ugly purple bruises on her wrist.

"What the hell?" I grabbed her arm and turned her wrist to inspect it. Those were definitely fingerprints. "Did Connor—"

"What? No!" She looked around. "It was one of the psych patients."

She answered quickly enough, and her answer made sense, but something flashed in her eyes before she pulled away.

"Look, if Connor hurt you—"

"Shh, no. I told you what happened, so drop it. Please."

No chance of that. Abi meant too much to me. The thought of someone hurting her made my gut clench. And it felt good, to feel something besides pain and grief. I wasn't going to drop it, but next time I mentioned it, I'd be taking it up with him. I'd despised Connor since the day I met him. The arrogant, overbearing doctor was totally wrong for her.

"Hey," Abi said. "Beep beep."

"I'm never going to live that down, am I?"

"Oh, God, no!" She grinned. "So, your Mom called. She wanted to know what I thought about having a surprise birthday party for you next week."

"Please tell me you shut that down."

She rolled her eyes. "Of course I did. I got your back, loser."

I thanked her and toyed with the saltshaker. "My mom calls you more than she calls me. I don't think she's ever given up on the idea of us together."

"Uh, excuse me. You should be so lucky."

"There's a problem with my eyes," I said. "I can't get them off you!"

She grinned, then made an 'ohhhh' sound. "I'm having a problem with mine, too, because I can't see you getting anywhere with me."

I'd had the distinct pleasure of sitting beside her at a bar one night when some guy had tried that on her and had been shot down in flames.

It felt good to laugh again, to hang out with Abi. But it also made me feel guilty. How could I laugh about anything, when my wife was dead?

After lunch, I went to check the

waiting room monitors. Everything seemed calm. I scanned all ten areas. Most everyone seemed to have bedded down for the night.

The TV still played on the third floor, but no one was watching. Three people slept while a fourth scrolled on his phone. As I watched, he laid his cell down and pulled the blanket over his head.

Opposite the recliners, in one of the chairs, something white and smoky rose. For a moment, I panicked, thinking 'fire.' But it didn't look like a fire. It looked like…someone standing. I gaped at the screen, and the thing seemed to take on a shape. It almost had a face, which it turned toward the guy with the cell. The TV winked off, pitching the room in darkness.

The televisions here were old. No remotes, no timers. To shut it off, a person had to physically touch it.

The guy's cell phone lit up. He held it over his head like a flashlight and scanned the room. Then he lay back down.

At that moment, Tony walked in.

"Dude," I said. "Watch this."

I replayed the video for him. He frowned, then watched it again. "That's just distortion in the tape."

"And the TV?"

He shrugged. "Maybe the power blinked."

Tony was one of the most practical people I'd ever known. He'd logic the hell out of this until he had a reasonable explanation. But he wasn't the one I really wanted to show this to. I wanted to show Abi.

"I'm going to walk around," I said, and he grabbed my arm.

"I have something for you." He pulled a small square of paper from his pocket. "Ambien. I thought you might want to try a couple and if it helps, get someone to write you some."

"Thanks."

I got in the elevator and went to the third floor to check that waiting room.

The people inside slept, and the TV remained off. I moved over to the chair, half-expecting something white and spectral rise from it. Nothing did, but the chair was not empty. A single daisy lay on the seat.

Unnerved, I took the elevator to Abi's floor. On my way to the nurses' desk, someone called to me from one of the rooms. I peeked inside, and the elderly woman on the bed motioned me closer.

"Ma'am? Can I help you with something?"

"I'm cold," she said. "Can you get me an extra blanket?"

I got one out of the closet and covered her.

"Thank you, dear. But what about her?"

"Who?" I asked, looking at the unoccupied bed on the other side.

She pointed behind me, at an empty corner.

"The girl in the pink gown says she's

cold, too."

I didn't say anything. Turning on my heel, I ran from the room. I forgot about Abi, forgot everything except how it felt to drag a beautiful, pale girl from a tub filled with hot water and blood, and how it had stained her white gown pink.

Somehow, I made it through the rest of the shift. I didn't care about the ghost in the waiting room, or the ghost in the old woman's room. I only worried about the ghost waiting for me at home. That's one reason I stopped by the gas station near home and picked up some beer.

My house didn't feel like a ghost lived here. It didn't feel like anyone did, myself included. I still didn't have a door on the bathroom, since I'd hauled the splintered one to the dump. I took the Ambien, drained three beers and climbed in the shower.

All I saw was her face. The pink, steaming water. Her gored wrist, and the one that wasn't, because she'd done such a great job on the first one she hadn't been able to finish the other.

I didn't need to be thinking of this before bed. I thought about staying up, but there had been too much of that lately. Yawning, I cut off the shower and grabbed a towel. After drying my face, I glanced at the mirror.

The words LET ME GO stood out on the mirror, scrawled on steamed glass.

It hit me like a punch. I didn't know how long it had been there, or if it was even real. I wandered to the kitchen in my boxers and peered out the window at Abi's house. Connor's Mustang sat in her drive. Glancing at my bedroom door, I couldn't go in there. Instead, I sat on the couch, finished the six pack and passed out.

***

I woke in my own bed after more dreams of my dead wife snuggling next to me, trying to escape the chill of her grave. Thankfully, the bedroom light was on.

The clock on the nightstand read 9:43. Panic froze me before I realised this was Monday, my day off. When I threw back the blanket, my heart stalled. Mud stained the bottom of my sheets, and my feet.

Grimy footprints covered my bedroom floor. My heart thumped painfully when I realised there were two sets. Mine leading into the room, and a smaller set going in both directions.

I didn't want to follow them because of what they might lead to, but I couldn't stand not knowing. I tracked them through the living room into the kitchen.

Food wrappers littered the counter. A half-empty peach Nehi sat on the marbled surface. Danae's favourite drink. I hated those things, but after she'd died, I hadn't been able to throw them out.

The footsteps led out the door. I hesitated, my hand on the knob, childishly afraid to step outside into the darkness. I glanced out the window at Abi's house.

Connor's Mustang still sat in the drive, parked next to her Camaro. But as I turned away, something caught my eye—a cigarette glowing in the darkness. I'd never known Abi to smoke. My curiosity superseded my fear of the dark, so I walked outside.

She jumped when I rapped on her window, then looked back at the house. She'd been crying, though she tried to hide her swollen eyes as she rolled the window down. All the crazy thoughts in my head dissipated like the smoke from her cigarette, replaced by concern.

"Abi, what's wrong?"

She began to cry. I jerked open the door and took her in my arms. She clung to me for a moment, then we heard Connor yell from inside.

"Go!" she said. "I'll be over in a little bit. I've got to end this my own way."

"You're breaking up with him?"

"Abigail!" Connor yelled.

I hated how he called her that, Abigail, like Abi wasn't good enough for him. Abi was too good for all of us. She shut the car door, dropped her cigarette in the drive and ground it with her heel. Then she did something that stunned me. She grabbed me and kissed me.

When she broke away, I stood there, paralyzed. She walked toward her house, then shot me a tremulous smile over her shoulder. "I have wanted to do that my entire life."

I didn't know what to do, so I walked

back to my house to wait. The sight of Danae's flowerbed stopped me in my tracks. All of the daisies had been dug up. Daisies and clumps of mud covered my lawn.

Had I done that?

Periodically, I glanced at Abi's house as I cleaned up the mess, then I showered. I didn't know what to think. Abi and I had never been like that. Not that I hadn't thought about it over the years. I mean, who wouldn't? Even though it felt like a betrayal, that kiss had felt right.

"Let me go."

Danae's voice startled me, clear as a bell in that empty living room. I turned, half-expecting to see her behind me. I grabbed our wedding photo off the wall and slammed it on the floor. Glass flew everywhere.

"YOU let *me* go!" I shouted. "You left me, Danae."

My cell rang. I grabbed it up, expecting Abi, but it was the hospital. Lanny, one of the night shift nurses, said, "I hate to bother you on your night off, but it's Mack. He's had a stroke and he's asking for you."

I didn't know what to do about Abi, so I sent her a text.

Mack's in intensive care. Headed to hospital

At the hospital, Lanny met me at the desk. "Glad you made it. I don't think he has long."

"Where is he?"

Of course. Exam room #3.

Mack's eyes were closed when I stepped around the curtain, but then he opened them and beckoned me.

"Danae," he rasped. He said something else, but I couldn't hear, so I leaned down. "Contract."

Then he died.

The word mystified me. What contract?

"Goodbye, Mack," I said, and walked outside.

I couldn't understand what was happening. I didn't know what Danae wanted from me, and sure as hell didn't know about any contract.

I caught the elevator and found myself outside the old lady's door, the one who'd mentioned the girl in the pink gown. If she'd talked to Danae once, maybe she could talk to her again. I knocked.

"Come in," she called.

"Ma'am, I don't know if you remember me—"

"You brought me a blanket," she said. "I'm not senile yet." I gave her a polite laugh, but my smile faded when she added, "The girl in the pink gown talks about you. She says your name is Jake."

"Did she say anything else?"

The old woman took my hand. "She said you have to let her go. She can't move on until you do."

"What does that mean?"

"She says there's a contract she can't break."

I shook my head. "I don't know anything about a contract. I don't know what she means."

"I'm sorry. I don't know."

I thanked her and left. Halfway to the parking lot, my cell phone rang. I fished it out of my pocket and froze when I saw the incoming caller ID.

Danae calling...

Her cell phone lay in a kitchen drawer, disconnected and dead for weeks now. I answered.

The crackle of static filled my ear, but the pounding of my pulse nearly drowned it out. A voice broke through, gritty and shrieking, but undeniably Danae.

"Hurry!" she screamed. "Abi!"

I jumped in my truck and tore out of

the parking lot.

Connor's car still sat in her driveway, but I didn't care. I took her front steps two at a time, then banged on her door. Something crashed. Fuelled by adrenaline, I jerked the knob and barrelled my way inside.

Connor straddled her on the living room floor, choking her. Abi's small hands beat ineffectively at him, her face an ugly mottled red. I grabbed him in a headlock and yanked him backwards. He let her go to defend himself, and Abi scuttled away.

We tumbled around her living room, trading blows and knocking over furniture. I finally found my feet and hauled him to his, jerking him out the front door. I tried to push him down the front steps, but he grabbed a fistful of my shirt and we both went.

Sirens screamed in the distance and soon strobing blue lights lit Abi's yard. Rough hands jerked us apart and they hauled both of us to the station.

Three hours later, I sat on Abi's steps, holding an ice pack to my eye and drinking a Jack and Coke.

"What happened?" I asked.

She didn't speak, and it took some prodding to get it out of her. They'd fought about me.

Abi had come home from the grocery store and found me passed out in Danae's flower bed. She'd helped me inside, inciting Connor's jealousy and rage. The second set of muddy footprints had belonged to her.

"I meant to come back over and help clean up," she said. "But things got a little crazy."

I didn't know what to say, so I simply squeezed her hand.

"I've known he was wrong for me for a long time, but I didn't want to admit it. I thought I could change him, but all I did was harm myself."

Harm myself...

Suddenly, I realised what contract Danae meant. I jumped up and said, "Abi, I'll explain everything in a little while, but I need to go find something."

"Can I help?" she asked.

"I think I have to do this alone. Can I come over later?"

"You better," she said.

It took me awhile, but I finally found it, tucked in a drawer of Danae's jewellery box. I lay across our bed to read it.

Danae's first suicide attempt had been in her teens, but her second had been about a year after we'd started dating. She'd told me about her battle with depression, but I'd never seen it coming, never had a clue how bad it was until I'd walked into that apartment that day and found her sprawled on the floor, empty prescription bottle in her hand. It'd been a close call that day, too.

A few days later, we'd been lying in her hospital bed together and I'd begged her to never do that again. She'd promised, then made a joke about drawing up a contract.

"I'd like that," I'd said, and she'd taken it more seriously than I'd thought. The next day, she'd presented me with this.

I, Danae Roberts, make a commitment to living. I will not harm myself or anyone else in any way. I will not attempt suicide, or any other self injury. If I begin to have thoughts of harming myself:

1) I will try to identify specifically what is upsetting me.

2) I will review alternatives to self-harm, such as thinking about my friends, family and my hot, supportive boyfriend, Jake

3) I will seek out a responsible, caring and supportive person if thoughts of self-harm continue.

4) If at this time I do not feel I can

control my behaviour, I will contact 911 or the nearest emergency room.

She'd signed it with a flourish, then made me witness and date it.

***

"I'm sorry you couldn't keep this promise," I said. "But you are no longer bound by it. I hope you find peace, Daisy."

I burned the contract over the bathroom sink and washed the ashes down the drain.

ABOUT THE PUBLISHER

BLACK HARE PRESS is a small, independent publisher based in Melbourne, Australia.

Founded in 2018, our aim has always been to champion emerging authors from all around the globe and offer opportunities for them to participate in speculative fiction and horror short story anthologies.

Connect

Website: *www.blackharepress.com*

Twitter: *@BlackHarePress*